MUNCHEM ACADEMY

2

THE GIRL WHO KNEW EVEN MORE

MUNCHEM ACADEMY

2

THE GIRL WHO KNEW EVEN MORE

COMMANDER S. T. BOLIVAR III

𝔇𝖎𝖘𝖓𝖊𝖞 • HYPERION

LOS ANGELES   NEW YORK

First Edition, October 2017
10 9 8 7 6 5 4 3 2 1
FAC-020093-17244
Printed in the United States of America

This book is set in 11.5 pt. CochinLTPro/Monotype; Somehand, Typewrither/
Fontspring
Designed by Phil Caminiti

Library of Congress Cataloging-in-Publication Data
    Names: Bolivar, S. T., III, author.
    Title: The girl who knew even more / by Commander S.T. Bolivar, III.
    Description: First edition. • Los Angeles : Disney-Hyperion, 2017. • Series:
        Munchem Academy ; book 2 • Summary: When strange weather occurs at his
        reform school, aspiring thief Mattie Larimore must save the world from
        chaos.
    Identifiers: LCCN 2017020404 • ISBN 9781484778579 (hardback)
    Subjects: CYAC: Reformatories—Fiction. • Schools—Fiction. •
        Weather—Fiction. • Science fiction. • Humorous stories. • BISAC: JUVENILE
        FICTION / Humorous Stories. • JUVENILE FICTION / Science Fiction. •
        JUVENILE FICTION / Mysteries & Detective Stories.
    Classification: LCC PZ7.1.B655 Gi 2017 • DDC [Fic]—dc23
    LC record available at https://lccn.loc.gov/2017020404

Reinforced binding
Visit www.DisneyBooks.com

SUSTAINABLE FORESTRY INITIATIVE Certified Sourcing
www.sfiprogram.org
SFI-00993

THIS LABEL APPLIES TO TEXT STOCK

FOR THE COMMANDER'S FATHER,

WHO ALWAYS BELIEVED

NEVER LET THEM SEE YOU PANIC

WELCOME TO ANOTHER BRILLIANT ACCOUNT OF MATHIAS LITTLETON Larimore's transformation into the world's greatest thief. While other biographers claim to know the truth about Mattie Larimore and how he eventually stole (and returned) the Great Pyramids, those biographers are wrong—and in the case of Sir Alistair Wicket, those biographers are also delusional, and still owe me twenty dollars.

Ahem. Yes, even the most inaccurate historian of criminal masterminds might cite how Mathias Littleton Larimore climbed the Canton Tower using only suction cups, but only the most talented know that when Mattie was twelve, he was small, he had no interest in suction cups, and he certainly had no idea he would grow up to be the world's greatest thief.

In fact, at this particular moment, Mattie wasn't entirely sure he was going to grow up at all, because Mr. Larimore's favorite scientists had invented the Aluminum Falcon and Mattie was about to try it.

"The Aluminum Falcon will revolutionize the way children travel!" Mr. Larimore bellowed to the crowd of reporters and students gathered on Munchem Academy's front lawn. Mattie's father stood on a hastily assembled metal stage, and every time he banged his wooden podium to emphasize a point, the metal planking clattered and whined. "No longer will you have to drive your child to soccer practice, rehearsals, or school! With the Aluminum Falcon, you simply program your destination and let your child *fly*!"

Fireworks exploded on either side of the stage, and an appreciative murmur rippled through the reporters. Whether they were appreciating the fireworks or the invention, Mattie wasn't sure. He was quite sure, however, he felt sick, maybe even more than a little sick, because the Aluminum Falcon didn't look like a revolution. It looked more like . . .

"A diaper," Carter Larimore muttered.

"A diaper that can make you fly," Mattie muttered back. He was trying to sound optimistic. He was fairly certain it wasn't working.

His brother quirked an eyebrow. "A diaper that can make you fly *and* catch on fire."

Definitely going to be sick, Mattie thought. He sat next to

Carter on a low-slung bench alongside the metal stage. They were supposed to look attentive and well-behaved in case the cameras panned to them. For Mattie, this meant putting his shoulders back and keeping his hands in his lap. For Carter, it meant trying to sleep with his eyes open.

"The Aluminum Falcon doesn't catch on fire anymore," Mattie whispered. "They tested it."

"You trust those two to test anything?" Carter jammed his thumb to their left. Mattie leaned forward and spotted Lem and Dr. Hoo standing at the crowd's edge. Lem was tall and narrow. Dr. Hoo was short and round. They were Larimore Corporation's chief scientists and very, *very* smart.

Lem had invented rapid-growing moss, but it fed on chipmunks, and Dr. Hoo had invented Always Flavorful Gum, but it choked the chewer, and they *both* had invented Wrinkles Away Cream, which totally worked because it ate the person's wrinkles . . . and most of the person's face.

Now that Mattie thought about it, most of Lem and Dr. Hoo's inventions ate, choked, or killed things.

Carter shook his head. "You're going to go down in history as the kid who crash-landed in a flaming diaper while screaming like a two-year-old."

It was not a visual Mattie needed and, of course, now he couldn't get it out of his mind. Truthfully, Mattie didn't want to go flying (or crashing) in the Aluminum Falcon, but he didn't want to disappoint his dad either. "Lem and Dr. Hoo are the company's lead inventors. Dad says they're really good at their jobs."

"Then why are they sweating so much?"

Carter was right: Lem and Dr. Hoo *were* sweating a lot. Lem kept patting his shiny forehead with a handkerchief and Dr. Hoo kept checking his swampy armpits.

It made Mattie's armpits go swampy too. "They look nervous. Why do they look nervous?"

"Maybe because they know they're about to barbecue the boss's son in front of the whole school?"

Mattie's stomach threatened to squeeze up his lunch.

"But the Aluminum Falcon won't be just any revolution," Mr. Larimore shouted. "It will be a *parental* revolution! No longer will you be shackled to your child's demanding schedule!"

The crowd clapped, and Mattie and Carter exchanged another look. It was a special look—one might even call it an understanding look—and for anyone who knew the brothers, it was also an unusual look, because until recently Carter always called Mattie girls' names and Mattie always considered Carter the bad brother. They had not gotten along, but then, somewhere between Carter getting cloned and Mattie rescuing him, things had taken a turn for the better.

It was complicated.

"Don't do it, Mattie. You'll catch on fire for sure."

"I promised Dad I would. It made him really happy."

Carter heaved an enormous sigh. "Still looks like a diaper."

"I agree." Caroline Spencer dropped onto the bench next to Mattie. Her dark eyes were huge in her moon-round face. "As your favorite—and smartest—best friend, I have to tell you: you're going to look like you're wearing your underwear over your pants."

Mattie thought for a moment. "Like a superhero?"

"Like a super dork." Mattie glared at her and Caroline shrugged. "I'm just sayin'."

"She's right," Carter agreed, nodding.

Technically, Caroline was almost always right. It was one of the many reasons she was Mattie's friend, and later, would be Mattie's partner in crime. In fact, Caroline would eventually know all the ways to turn boots, pants, and hamsters into Aluminum Falcons, but right now she thought the idea was ridiculous.

"And now!" Up on the stage, Mr. Larimore rubbed his hands together. "Without further ado, I give you . . . the Aluminum Falcon!"

Carter shook his head. "Please don't shriek like a girl on your way down."

"And please don't scream like a boy when you hit the dirt," Caroline added.

Mattie glared at them, but Caroline and Carter didn't notice because they were too busy glaring at each other. Mattie patted his sweaty palms against his pants and stood up.

He walked across the grass to the stage steps and joined his father and Lem by the podium.

"Stop looking like you're going to throw up," Lem whispered.

"But I *feel* like I'm going to throw up."

"Well, pretend like you don't. Your mother's an actress, so, you know, *act*." Lem held out the Aluminum Falcon. Up close, the "parental revolution" looked even less like anything "aluminum" and way more like a diaper. The fabric was concrete gray with coffee can–size engines on either hip, and there were big red buttons down the butt.

"Do I want to know what those do?" Mattie asked.

Lem took an awfully long moment to think about it.

"Never mind." Mattie tugged the Falcon on over his pants and fastened the connector just below his belt. It wasn't exactly uncomfortable, but it was kind of warm.

Like really warm.

"Uh, Lem?" Mattie shimmied his butt from side to side, but it didn't help. His butt still felt like it was being slowly cooked. "Why's it hot?"

"That's the jet pack," Lem explained, his long brown fingers tapping something into the Aluminum Falcon's control pad.

"Is it going to get worse?"

"Of course not. We tested it."

Carter's earlier words echoed in Mattie's head and his armpits broke out in a fresh sweat.

"And now!" Mattie's father boomed, and his microphone screeched. "For the moment you've all been waiting for! My son, Mathias Littleton Larimore, will demonstrate the full power of the Aluminum Falcon!"

This was Mattie's cue to smile and wave at the audience. The audience did not smile or wave back.

Which made Mattie's father frown.

Mr. Larimore was a short, wide man, and perhaps because he was so short and wide, he liked big things: big SUVs, big buildings, big corporations. At the moment, Mr. Larimore loved his big podium because when no one smiled back at his son, Mr. Larimore could pound on it and make the microphone screech.

"The Aluminum Falcon!" he bellowed, and this time people cheered.

"Okay," Lem whispered, backing up a step. "I've already programmed the coordinates for a spin around the school. If that doesn't work, I'll control the Falcon manually—"

"And if *that* doesn't work?" Mattie interrupted.

Lem thought about it. "It'll work. It *will*."

"Are you convincing me or you?"

Lem didn't answer. He showed Mattie a small yellow remote control. It fit perfectly in Mattie's palm. "If you get nervous, just press this button here and it will radio me." The scientist patted Mattie's shoulder. "We'll handle everything. You just smile."

Mattie nodded. He knew this part, and he would try his best, but the thing was, it was awfully hard to try his best when the Aluminum Falcon was pinching his butt and the waistband was making it hard to breathe—or perhaps that was just an effect of being stared at. The crowd was so quiet. All eyes were pinned to Mattie.

Lem took Mr. Larimore's spot behind the podium and opened a slim silver laptop. After a few keystrokes, the Aluminum Falcon's engines cut on with a whine and a sputter, pushing Mattie up a few inches and then a few more. His sneakers dangled in the air.

"Ready?" Lem yelled over the engines' roar.

Mattie nodded and Lem pushed another series of buttons on the keyboard. Nothing happened. Lem pushed a few more buttons. Still nothing. Lem walloped the side of the computer and the Falcon jerked.

Uh-oh, Mattie thought, but he didn't think it for long because the Falcon suddenly surged upward, shooting sparks into the grass.

NEVER LET THEM SEE YOU PANIC— UNLESS YOU *NEED* TO PANIC, IN WHICH CASE, GO AHEAD AND SCREAM. A LOT.

THE ALUMINUM FALCON SHIFTED AGAIN, PICKING UP SPEED. MATTIE glimpsed his brother's face as he powered higher. "Don't puke," Carter called.

I'm totally going to puke, Mattie thought, squeezing his eyes shut. Cold air whipped over his cheeks as the Aluminum Falcon climbed and climbed.

And jerked to a stop.

Mattie popped open his eyes. He was hundreds of feet above the crowd now. Lem had told him everyone would look like ants at this height, but to Mattie, their faces were more like shiny blobs. Everyone was staring at him.

"Okay," Lem's voice squeaked through the radio at Mattie's hip. "You ready to show them what the Falcon can do?"

Mattie took a deep, *deep* breath and pressed the radio's response button. "Yep."

Pssshfffttt. Pssshfffttt. The Aluminum Falcon began to climb again. It went faster and faster and then suddenly dipped. Mattie's stomach soared into his throat. The Falcon pivoted and Mattie's stomach twirled. The Falcon went into a dive and Mattie flung his arms wide.

It's like riding a roller coaster! he thought as the Falcon swooped him higher.

"You okay?" Lem asked and the radio crackled. "You're not scared, are you?"

"No, no, I'm really good!" Mattie waved to the crowd and the crowd waved back and, this time, Mattie didn't have to fake his grin. "This is amazing, Lem."

Maybe even more than amazing because this high, the air was sweeter and colder, the tops of the trees looked like dark green bottle brushes, and the Munchem cemetery looked . . . well, if not exactly pretty, it certainly looked prett*er* than it usually did. The spiny black iron fence didn't seem quite so sharp and the long yellowy weeds didn't seem quite so long and yellowy.

The Munchem roof still looks terrible, Mattie thought as he spun in a circle, taking in the whole school. Lem and Dr. Hoo were geniuses! The Aluminum Falcon was so much *fun*!

Until it wasn't.

The Falcon jerked, heaving Mattie a few feet higher, then dipping him so low and so fast his head snapped back.

Putputputput. Pow!

Mattie's knees nearly hit his face, his arms whipped from side to side, and far, far below, he heard Mr. Larimore's microphone squeal.

"Just look at the Falcon's maneuverability!" Mattie's dad bellowed as his son's knees snapped upward again. "Notice the lightning-fast reflexes!"

Mattie noticed them all right. He fumbled with the radio remote. "Uh, Lem?"

"On it."

"Thanks—"

ScreeeeeeeeeeePOP!

The Falcon dropped a couple feet and smoke streamed from the waistband. Mattie coughed. His eyes watered, turning everything smeary and shimmery.

"There!" Lem said, and the Falcon leveled out. "Sorry. I'm going to put it on manual controls. How's that?"

"Better." Mattie jammed his thumb against the radio button again. "Yes. Yes, this is better."

Or was it? Because now Mattie was hovering just above Munchem Academy's thick forest. The tops of trees brushed his sneakers like fingers stretching for the sun, and when a cool breeze whisked past, it peeled back brown leaves and piney branches. Mattie spotted a squirrel nest . . . a cardinal . . . a pair of red eyes.

Red eyes?! Mattie blinked and looked again. A pale, bony hand wound up through the leaves! It was reaching for his foot!

The Aluminum Falcon dropped.

"Aiiiiiieeeeeeee!" Mattie screeched as he swooshed past the eyes, the hand, and approximately 2,565,284 branches. He plunged toward the ground.

I'mgoingtodie!

Ka—POW!!

Once again, the Falcon stopped. The engines repositioned their directions and pushed Mattie through the tree limbs. One of the branches caught him in the face and he spit out a leaf.

"Hold on," Lem said. He sounded rather breathless. Mattie could relate. His heart was jackhammering in his chest. The Falcon pushed him out of the forest, shifted, and began to lower. It lowered and lowered until finally . . .

Whump.

Mattie hit the lawn and blinked up at the bright blue sky. He couldn't catch his breath and his butt hurt, but nothing felt broken.

And nothing was on fire.

"Mattie!" Lem rushed to Mattie's side and dropped to his knees. The scientist's eyes bugged behind his glasses. "Talk to me!"

"I'm okay." Mattie sat up and shook grass clippings out of his hair. He'd landed only twenty or so feet from the stage and audience. Caroline was ashen-faced, Carter didn't look surprised, and Mr. Larimore? Well, Mr. Larimore's big blue forehead vein was pulsing.

"Your father is going to fire me," Lem said, using the same tone one would use for observing how grass is green or how daggers stab people in the back. He was resigned to his fate.

But Mattie wasn't. "No way," he whispered as Mr. Larimore stomped toward them. "Follow my lead."

"What?"

"Act like you're not terrified!" Mattie bounced to his feet and flung his arms wide, grass bits flying everywhere. He grinned at the reporters. "Ta-da!"

The reporters stared and said nothing and Lem stared and said nothing. Mattie nudged the scientist with his toe.

"Oh! Ta-da!" Lem managed.

"What are you doing?" Mr. Larimore hissed. His short, round shadow slipped over Mattie and Lem.

"That sure was fun!" Mattie cried. He struggled out of the Aluminum Falcon and held it above his head like a trophy. "Who wants to go next?"

The crowd shifted but no one said anything, and the silence stretched so long Mattie began to sweat and Lem began to shake.

"Sit down!" Mr. Larimore said, his blue forehead vein still pulsing. Nothing good ever happened when Mr. Larimore's vein pulsed. Sometimes people got fired. Sometimes people cried. Either way, there was always a lot of screaming and running around. "Go sit down right now, Mattie!"

Mattie went to sit down. He gave the Falcon back to Lem and crossed the lawn, feeling the crowd's eyes following him. No one was impressed—and why would they be? The Aluminum Falcon was a disaster, and Mattie Larimore was a very small, very average twelve-year-old. To anyone else, he looked forgettable.

Thankfully I am not anyone else, and to me Mattie looked precisely like the pint-size version of the criminal he would eventually grow up to be.

Perhaps a bit more bedraggled—definitely a bit more singed—than he would be after the Great Pyramid Swap, but I can see the promise, the possibility, THE MENACE HE WILL ONE DAY BE!

Ahem.

Yes, it was going to be another promising chapter in young Mattie's life, and if he had known what I know, he would've been terrified.

Or excited.

Mostly terrified.

But the important thing is *I'm* excited because *this* is another chapter in Mattie Larimore the Thief's great beginning, which means it's also another chapter in Mattie Larimore the Good Boy's horrible ending.

Don't say you weren't warned.

SOMETIMES YOU FLY, AND SOMETIMES YOU FALL, AND SOMETIMES YOU DON'T KNOW WHAT YOU'LL DO UNTIL YOU DO IT

AH, MUNCHEM ACADEMY. WITH ITS THREE AND A HALF TOWERS, four stories, twenty-two fireplaces, and secret basement hiding a machine you could clone yourself with, it's the perfect place for not-so-perfect children—and perhaps not-so-perfect inventions too.

"What a disaster," Mattie muttered, picking grass out of his teeth. It tasted a bit like one of his mother's green smoothies. Actually, the grass was better, but not by much.

"Don't sweat it," Caroline whispered. She was leaning forward to listen to Mr. Larimore, both hands wrapped around her backpack straps like she was going to parachute away. "This whole thing could have gone way worse."

"How's that possible?"

"You could be dead."

Sadly, Mattie had to admit this was true. He rubbed his still-tingling left eyebrow. "At least I didn't scream, much."

"We were all very proud." Caroline crammed her elbow into Carter's side. "Weren't we?"

Carter winced. "Very."

"Guys," Mattie began, "there's more. I saw—"

"I'm ready for your questions!" Mr. Larimore bellowed into his microphone. "You there!" Mattie's father pointed to a woman close to the stage. She was tall and blond and, when she threw her shoulders back, it made her look like she belonged on the prow of a ship. "What's your question?"

"Why the sudden interest in our nation's youth, Mr. Larimore?" The reporter held up a small black recorder. "Larimore Corporation has never shown any interest in children before. What changed?"

"Oh! Oh! I know this one!" The voice came from the back. Someone tried to shush him, but the man would not be shushed. A familiar red head bobbed into view.

"Thank you, Headmaster Rooney," Mr. Larimore said, forehead vein throbbing once more. "I'll take this question."

"But I know the answer!"

Mr. Larimore ignored him. "And you are, Miss . . . ?"

"Boar," the reporter said, "Liv St. Boar."

"Ah, yes." For the briefest of seconds, Mr. Larimore

frowned. "You're the one who wrote about our recent successes in kitchen innovation."

"Is that what we're calling pizza dough that turns blue when heated? A success?"

Mr. Larimore frowned again. "Every business has setbacks, Miss St. Boar, but at Larimore Corporation we look to the future—and *children*? Children *are* the future, so luckily for everyone, Munchem Academy is poised to deliver them."

"But I thought Munchem was a school for bad children?"

Mr. Larimore's smile pushed wide. "Don't you believe in second chances?"

"I do! I do!" It was Headmaster Rooney again. Carter started laughing.

"Stop it," Caroline hissed. "You know he's still not himself."

Carter did indeed know that. In fact, it was rather Carter's fault the headmaster wasn't himself—well, Carter's and Mattie's and the Spencers'. Carter shrugged. "You should be thanking me. The Rooster hasn't strung anyone up by the ankles in months. *Months!* It's a real live miracle."

Or the effects of being locked in a cloning pod set to Turbo, Mattie thought. The Rooster hadn't really been the Rooster since—not that Mattie knew anything about cloning pods and Turbo settings and headmasters who had suddenly lost their memories.

Correction: not that Mattie would *admit* he knew anything about that.

After all, how would Mattie explain that Headmaster Rooney had been so sick of Munchem's bad kids that he decided to clone them and give the new and improved clones back to the parents while the real kids wasted away in special pods? And *then* how would Mattie explain that he found the cloning machine? And stopped it? But not before Carter was cloned?

The short answer? He couldn't. So he kept his mouth shut and swore he had no idea why the headmaster was so very . . . ah . . . happy.

In the meantime, Mr. Larimore was helping Headmaster Rooney "get Munchem on track," which mostly seemed to mean Mr. Larimore improved the school and then invited reporters in to look at the improvements. Mattie's dad called it "good publicity." Carter called it "annoying."

"Sure, these kids made mistakes," Mr. Larimore continued, patting his shirt's straining buttons. "But thanks to my company's funding, Munchem is gaining a new roof, a new gym, new science programs—all in this beautiful, quiet countryside setting."

"Where no one can hear us scream," Carter whispered.

Mattie shuddered. He couldn't help it. Carter always said that, but it didn't make the saying any less true. Munchem *was* in the middle of nowhere, and as it turned out, the middle of nowhere was an excellent place for stashing bad kids.

And, apparently, testing out Aluminum Falcons.

"At Munchem Academy," Mr. Larimore continued, pointing at the crowd with a single, thick finger, "the best you is a *new* you!"

The students stared straight ahead—they'd heard the motto way too much to be impressed—but the reporters exchanged a suspicious look, and Liv St. Boar's look might have been the most suspicious of all. Mattie didn't blame her. After last term, Munchem's motto made him twitchy and suspicious too. He glanced toward the thick forest that surrounded the school's bright green fields. Three months ago, the teachers and clones had escaped, but every once in a while, Mattie thought he saw red eyes flashing behind the dark trees.

After today, he was sure of it.

"I saw one of the clones," Mattie whispered. Caroline and Carter froze and, after a pause, turned toward him. "When the Falcon nearly stuck me in the tree," he explained. "I saw red eyes and then a hand grabbed for me."

Caroline paled. "Are you sure?"

Mattie nodded. "I thought all the clones escaped with the teachers. I don't know why some of them would still be in the woods."

"Who cares?" Carter asked, watching Mr. Larimore pound on his podium some more. Their father was explaining how the Larimore Corporation was going to lead the future, and the reporters were nodding along.

"Poor things. It's not like they have anywhere else to

go." Caroline gnawed at the skin around her thumbnail. "What else were they going to do? Miss Maple just up and left."

"Miss Maple." Carter savored the name like a piece of candy. "She seemed so sweet."

And indeed Carter was right. Miss Maple had seemed sweet. The school secretary was blond and pillowy and had a smile for everyone—and behind that smile she had been plotting to clone all the students.

"What if she's back?" Carter asked suddenly. A couple of reporters glanced their way and Carter gave them two thumbs up. "She vowed revenge on us for spoiling her plans."

"No way," Caroline whispered. "Miss Maple wouldn't dare come back here, and the clones weren't into revenge—remember how nice Doyle was?" She paused, face screwing up in thought. "I still can't figure out how he managed to make those pumpkin muffins in his dorm room."

Carter rolled his eyes. "One of life's great mysteries."

Caroline kicked him and Carter flinched.

"Stop it," Mattie whispered. "We have to figure out what we're going to do."

"Do? I'm not doing anything." Carter rubbed his shin. "I'm going to keep pretending I have no idea what's out there."

"But we *do* know what's out there."

"I am not explaining how I know that," Carter said. "Leave the clones alone. Live and let live, you know?"

Up on the stage, Mr. Larimore held up the Aluminum

Falcon and gestured to its coffee can–size engines. "Now, if you will just take a closer look—"

"Oh, I think we've seen enough," Liv St. Boar said, tossing her tiny recorder into her equally tiny purse. "In fact, I think we've seen *plenty*."

The other reporters seemed to agree. They were pushing back their plastic lawn chairs and standing up. They were ready to leave. Mr. Larimore's face went white with panic. "But, wait! There's more!"

No one waited, no one wanted more, and Mattie felt bad for Lem all over again. The scientist was slumped at the stage edge, watching Mr. Larimore, whose forehead vein was still pulsing. It looked like a squirmy blue worm pinned to his face.

"Whatever you're thinking about the clones, *don't*," Carter repeated before melting into the crowd.

Mattie watched him go. "I still think we should do something," he muttered.

"I don't." Caroline stood and brushed off her sweater. It was covered in brown Beezus fur. Her lab rat was molting. Again. "C'mon, we'll ask Eliot—but he's going to agree with me."

Mattie wasn't so sure. In fact, he started to tell Caroline precisely that and stopped.

"What is it?" Caroline asked.

"Nothing." But it was something, because Mattie felt a prickling on his skin, a spray of goose bumps between his shoulder blades, and, frankly, an itching in his teeth.

Many years later, Mattie would feel this same something before being ambushed by pirates. It was his intuition, and it would save his life many times over. But right now? Well, right now, Mattie thought his teeth were just itchy. He didn't know anything about pirates or intuition or why fortune cookies always taste stale.

And he definitely, *definitely* didn't know someone was watching him.

REMEMBER YOUR STORY AND STICK TO IT

"STOP PICKING YOUR TEETH, MATTIE!" CAROLINE COVERED HER EYES with one hand. It didn't do much good. She still had to peek through her fingers to keep from running into the hallway lockers. "I don't want to see that!"

"Then stop looking at me," Mattie told her, picking harder. They turned up a set of stairs and took the steps two at a time. "I don't know what's wrong with me. They're all itchy."

Caroline shoved open the double doors to the science wing. "Maybe you're developing allergies."

The hallway was noonday bright and the overhead lights buzzed like wasps. Last term, the wing smelled like cleaning fluid and body odor. Today, it smelled like—

"Is that roasted turkey?" Mattie asked.

"Yes." Caroline pulled her Munchem sweater up over her mouth and nose. "And it's disgusting."

Mattie sniffed, and sniffed again. "I think it's kind of nice — way nicer than the pumpkin pie scent they tried last week. That stuff smelled like a dirty hamster cage."

"Yeah, Lem said it ended up being their most successful scent though."

"Really? How'd you find that out?"

"He was reviewing the data during study hall and got all excited. He wanted to share. The stink increased student productivity by thirty-two percent."

Mattie stared at Caroline.

"I know, right? It's because everyone wanted to hurry up and get away from the smell, so they worked really fast. Lem said Dr. Hoo is going to try the moldy laundry scent at the Larimore headquarters next week. He says it could be a great breakthrough in worker productivity."

"Moldy laundry scent?"

"Yeah, you know, like when you forget laundry in the washer and it smells all gross when you finally find it?"

"Oh, yeah. Hope they don't try it on us."

"They'll probably come up with something worse."

Mattie couldn't fault Caroline's observation. Ever since the Larimore Corporation had taken over Munchem, new experiments happened every day. Sometimes, it was special scents being pumped through the school's air ducts. Sometimes, it was moss that ate chipmunks. It was always a surprise though, and then every Friday, the students answered questionnaires about how the experiments made them feel.

And whether they would buy those products.

It was supposed to help Larimore scientists with their research. As far as Mattie could tell, it really just helped the students get out of the last twenty minutes of American History.

Caroline stopped at the first classroom door and banged on the glass. There was a scuffle from inside and the door cracked open. A sliver of Eliot's face appeared.

Like Caroline, Eliot Spencer was also Mattie's best friend and destined to be his future partner in crime. It was thanks to Eliot's computer knowledge that Mattie was able to figure out how to stop Rooney's clones. The solution had involved a little bit of breaking and entering, a little more sneaking around, and rather a lot of overloading the clones and making them dance.

Eliot looked at Mattie. "I can't believe you nearly died in a diaper."

"I can't believe you missed it," Caroline said.

"Yeah." Eliot frowned. "Professor Shelley said missing the assembly would really teach me not to reset her passwords."

Mattie and Caroline exchanged a look. "And did it?" Mattie asked Eliot.

"No."

Caroline rubbed her forehead like she was developing a headache. "Are you done with detention?"

"I hope not."

Caroline rubbed her forehead harder. "I worry about you, you know that?"

Frankly, Mattie was starting to worry too. Eliot was trying to impress their technology teacher. Like Lem and Dr. Hoo, Professor Shelley was a Larimore Corporation scientist. Unlike Lem and Dr. Hoo, Professor Shelley wasn't known for inventions that ate things. She was known for big computers, and bigger robots.

"Don't ruin this for me," Eliot whispered. "I'm making progress with her."

"Eliot? Who's there?" Professor Shelley appeared at the door. Tall and thin, she loved every color in the rainbow as long as it was black. "Oh. Hello, Mattie. Very glad you survived."

"Me too."

"Is your father quite upset?"

Mattie thought about the pulsing blue vein and tried not to shudder. "You could say that. Can Eliot go now?"

Professor Shelley checked her watch. It was wider than her wrist and the digital display always made her thin face go monster green. "Good heavens, yes. You could've left ten minutes ago, Eliot."

Eliot frowned.

"You'll do better tomorrow, right?" Professor Shelley added, pulling her cardigan tighter.

"Probably not," Eliot said.

At least he's honest, Mattie thought.

Professor Shelley looked at Eliot as if she were sucking on a sour candy. "Go to class," she said, and shoved Eliot into the hallway.

The door slammed shut in Eliot's face and he frowned. "Professor Shelley just doesn't appreciate what I bring to the table."

"Like what?"

"Computer viruses mostly." Eliot scratched the side of his neck. "I'm going to override her computer tomorrow. She'll be really impressed."

"Somehow I don't think that's the word you're looking for."

"Amazed?"

"Nope."

"Thrilled?"

Mattie didn't answer. He grabbed Eliot's arm and dragged him after his sister.

The science wing might have been turkey-scented, but the lower floor English classes smelled like buttery scones with raspberry jam, and Mattie's stomach growled as he pushed his way through the other students. He tried to concentrate on

Eliot's play-by-play of his detention, but Mattie couldn't ignore the whispers of "totally ate dirt" and "diaper" as he passed the other students.

"I'm never going to live down the Aluminum Falcon thing, am I?" Mattie asked.

Eliot scrunched his nose up in confusion. "What? Oh. No, I don't think Professor Shelley cares."

"Hey, Little Larimore!" someone shouted.

Mattie cringed. Little Larimore? The nickname was even worse than when Carter called him dog names for an entire semester. Mattie stared straight ahead. *Please don't be me. Please don't be me.*

Mattie knew it was a useless prayer. After all, he was a Larimore, and let's face it, quite little.

"I'm talking to *you*, Little Larimore!"

Mattie and the Spencers turned. Doyle was galloping in their direction.

"Oh. *No*," Mattie whispered, feeling his eyes bug wide. Doyle had been Mattie's roommate since last semester. Everything about the other boy was big: big head, big fists, big body—and an even bigger interest in holding down smaller kids and spitting in their mouths.

Doyle grabbed Mattie by his collar. "I was talking to you!"

Mattie's head went a little fuzzy with panic. "Hey, Doyle," he managed as Doyle dragged him closer. "I didn't realize you meant me. How you doing?"

"Better than you." Doyle released Mattie's collar and Mattie rocked back on his heels. "Your dad's all right. If we have assemblies like that every week, this place will be way more entertaining."

Mattie wasn't sure what to say to that, but he needn't have worried because Doyle spotted his best friend, Maxwell, and galloped off in the opposite direction. Mattie rubbed his throat.

"Little Larimore," Caroline repeated, scratching her stomach. Beneath her sweater, Beezus wiggled in appreciation. "It's not bad—better than some of the stuff Carter's called you."

"Not by much." Mattie winced as Doyle tackled Maxwell. They began to wrestle, crashing into sixth graders and lockers. "He's in a good mood."

"Probably made one of the teachers cry again," Caroline added.

Mattie's stomach squeezed. Seeing Real Doyle crashing about made him think about Clone Doyle, who enjoyed baking. Mattie started to open his mouth, and Caroline held up one hand.

"I know what you're thinking," she said, and just before they reached the classroom door, Caroline stopped and turned to face both boys. "Mattie has something he wants to tell you," she said to her brother.

Eliot looked at Mattie.

Mattie looked around in case any of the other students

were paying attention. "I saw a clone," he whispered. "In the woods."

Eliot clasped both hands together. "For reals?"

"Yeah. It was up in the trees like it was trying to grab me. The eyes were all red."

"He thinks we should do something about them," Caroline added, tugging one hand through her knotted hair. It was looking especially windblown today. The dark tangles climbed toward the ceiling like Lem's moss crawled toward chipmunks.

"Of course we should do something!" Eliot's eyes went bright. "I've always wanted to take one of those things apart. We could do that!"

"Not really what I had in mind," Mattie told him. The hallway was growing more crowded by the minute. The scones-and-jam scent was starting to be tinged with the smell of student.

"What else would you want with them?" Eliot asked.

"To make sure they don't tell anyone about what Rooney did?" Mattie listed off reasons on his fingers. "To make sure they don't tell anyone about what *we* did? To make sure my dad doesn't get in trouble because the cloning machine was made entirely with Larimore Corporation *parts*? Take your pick. We have to do something!"

Eliot put a hand on his friend's sleeve. "Let me ask you a few questions, Mattie. Are those woods out of bounds?"

"Well, yeah."

"Are those clones murderous?"

Mattie blinked. "Not particularly."

"Then why were the clone's eyes red?"

Mattie thought about this. Eliot had a good point. Typically, the clones' eyes only turned red when they were stressed or mad. The rest of the time they looked like everyone else. The clone in the tree? He'd been agitated.

Eliot smirked. "See what I mean?"

"*No*, because murderous clones hiding in the woods is definitely something people need to know about."

Eliot sighed. "Look, Mattie. You gotta stick to our story. We can't tell the truth now."

Mattie scowled at the Spencers and the Spencers scowled at Mattie. Then Mattie thought about what Eliot said and it made him scowl even more. Eliot had another good point.

"We've let the whole thing go on for too long," Caroline said.

"Plus," Eliot added, dropping his voice, "there's what we did to Rooney. I don't want to explain that to the police or my mom."

"Ugh." Caroline's nose wrinkled. "Agreed."

Mattie opened his mouth and Caroline thumped him. "If we tell, they'll close Munchem."

"And throw us in prison," Eliot said. Mattie and Caroline looked at him and he shrugged. "What? You don't know. It's not like this has happened to anyone else."

Caroline and Mattie had to admit this was true.

"Besides," Eliot continued. "Those woods are creepy and I've seen all the movies. You go into them to save the day? You won't come back out."

ALWAYS REMEMBER TO LOOK UP

MOST RESEARCHERS DON'T FAULT ELIOT SPENCER ON THIS ONE.
People usually don't come out of dark forests, dilapidated old
houses, and certain dentists' offices. So what should you do
when confronted with one? Avoid it. Just turn around and go
elsewhere. It's simply a good principle to live by. Other exam-
ples include never wearing black and navy, never combining
dinosaur DNA, and never *ever* accepting a mysterious invita-
tion to a reclusive billionaire's remote island. Take my word for
it, it won't end well.

Now where were we? Oh, yes, Mattie and the Spencers were
on their way to American history class. They rushed through
the door just as the late bell chimed and took their usual seats
by the windows that overlooked Munchem's new gym. Or,

more accurately, the windows that overlooked Munchem's new gym that was never used for gym class because it had been commandeered by Larimore scientists.

Caroline leaned close to the glass. "They're planting flowers again."

Mattie leaned close as well. Two stories below, Larimore employees lugged buckets of leafy plants around. It looked like they were trying—and failing—to find sunny spots. The ballroom-turned-gym-turned-lab was covered in hulking gargoyles. They cast uneven shadows everywhere.

"I don't know why they bother planting anything," Mattie said. "Everything they put there dies. It's just like the gardens."

"It's creepy," Caroline said.

"I think it's nice some things stay the same," Eliot said, settling into his desk. "Nothing else has around here."

It was true. Last term, the mansion shed roof tiles, the hallways were always dirty, and the windows were cloudy with fingerprints. This term, things were cleaner and things were fixed—or getting fixed in the case of the roof, which seemed to be making the repair team use every swear word they knew.

Even Carter was impressed.

Bottom line, aside from Mattie nearly being turned into a lawn dart, Munchem Academy was starting to be very academy-like.

"Do you think Lem is going to make it?" Eliot asked, staring down the beige-faced clock above the whiteboard. "Because if your dad has decided to fire him or melt him down for parts or whatever, I don't want to wait around."

Mattie frowned. He wasn't sure. When it came to Mr. Larimore anything was possible, and as Mattie was considering it, Doyle and Maxwell strolled into class. The bigger boys dropped into their seats, which squeaked in protest. Or maybe that was just Maxwell. Doyle had put him in a headlock again.

"I hope Lem gets here soon," Caroline whispered as Maxwell's eyes bugged.

Personally, Mattie doubted Lem would be able to stop Doyle. In addition to being one of Larimore Corporation's lead scientists, Lem was also one of Munchem Academy's newest teachers—and possibly the quietest. He was definitely the nicest.

These were great qualities, but not necessarily useful in a person who was supposed to keep Doyle from spitting on people.

The late bell rang and Lem surged through the classroom's door. The tall, thin scientist dropped an armful of papers onto his desk and smeared them around. None of the other students noticed his arrival. They were too busy watching Doyle and Maxwell trying to kill each other.

"Sorry the demonstration went wrong, Lem," Mattie said.

"It didn't go wrong," Lem said, running one hand along his black hair. Smoke steamed from it, and Mattie really, *really* wanted to ask what had happened. "I figured out a way to do it that doesn't work. There's a difference."

"But not by much," Eliot whispered. His sister kicked him and Eliot yelped.

Lem didn't seem to notice. He flipped some papers around. "It's all in how you look at it," he explained. "Remember the Goo-B-Gone experiment?"

"Couldn't forget it if I tried," Mattie said—and it was true. No one would forget that experiment. While Mattie's old teachers, Mr. Karloff and Mrs. Hitchcock, had mostly been interested in cloning bad students and teaching the rest of them to clean, Lem was interested in teaching his classes about the periodic table, the difference between acids and bases, and to never, ever mix hydrochloric acid with Larimore Corporation's Dirt-B-Doomed Starter Solution.

Even when Lem said they should.

"Ah, yes," Lem had said at the time, watching the thick pink liquid dissolve Mattie's desktop (and seconds later the linoleum floor). "I'd forgotten about that."

Mattie had taken a step back, the fumes stinging his eyes. "You forgot? How could you forget?"

"I have a lot on my mind." Lem had peered down at the widening hole, studying the newly exposed pipes and then the newly developed holes in the pipes. "Though maybe I've just discovered a new technique for making windows and doorways."

That was Lem. Always optimistic.

And thanks to that optimistic new technique, Lem was no longer allowed to teach sixth-grade science.

"Okay, everyone." Lem cleared his throat, and patted his black hair. Gray tendrils of smoke swirled into a halo above his head. "Open your books to chapter forty-eight. We're going to continue our discussion on the events leading up to the Civil War."

HummmmmNAH!

The window air-conditioning unit turned on, flooding the room with icy air. It pushed away the scent of scones and jam and replaced it with the scent of . . . rain?

Mattie sniffed and then sniffed again. Yep, it smelled like rain. The air conditioner blew a little harder, ruffling Mattie's hair. He rolled his shoulders, glanced toward the ceiling, and . . .

What is that? Mattie thought. There were swirly, soft wisps circling the plaster ceiling. They seemed to be coming through the air vent and they were gathering closer and closer. They looked almost like a cloud.

Impossible, Mattie thought.

"Let's begin," Lem said.

Booooom! something went. It sounded like a far-off roar. Everyone paused. They looked at each other, and then they looked around, and then they looked up. Just in time to see streams of water pour down. *Cold* water.

"Argh!" everyone cried. "The sprinklers!"

Mattie squinted against the water running in his eyes. The white plaster and dark beams were hidden behind that foggy, wispy gray mass. It still looked like a cloud and now it rained like a cloud.

But it *can't* be a cloud, Mattie thought, his eyes still glued to the ceiling. Water soaked through his clothes, dripping all the way to socks and underwear. *We're inside.*

Mattie started to ask the Spencers if either of them were seeing what he was seeing and realized the Spencers weren't seeing anything. Well, they weren't looking *up*. Eliot was scrambling to cover his computer manuals and Caroline was shielding Beezus. No one was looking at the ceiling.

Well, no one was looking at the ceiling except for Lem.

Water ran down Lem's cheeks and dribbled off his black hair and *still* he did not look away from the ceiling. His face was scrunched tight like he was thinking.

Boom! Boom! The lights flickered, flashing the room pale pink. Someone screamed. It sounded like Doyle.

"Everybody out!" Lem shouted. He pointed one finger at the door. "Now! Go!"

And everyone went, but not fast enough.

BOOM! The books trembled on their shelves and the whole sixth-grade history class surged forward, shoes squeaking on the wet tiles. Doyle squeezed through the door first and ran down the hallway, arms pinwheeling.

Thunder, Mattie thought. *It sounds* exactly *like thunder.* "What is going—"

"C'mon, Mattie!" Caroline dug her fingers into Mattie's

arm as pink light lit the classroom again. Something popped and the overhead lights showered them in tiny glass bits. "Do you *want* to get electrocuted?"

Mattie did not, and as another round of pink light exploded above them, he raced Caroline out the door and into the scone-and-jam-scented hallway.

SOMETIMES YOU HAVE TO SEE IT
TO BELIEVE IT

MATTIE AND CAROLINE RAN PAST THE LOCKERS AND BURST THROUGH
the heavy wooden doors at the top of the steps. Sunshine
blinded them and Mattie skidded to a stop, his wet shoes slip-
ping on the dry stone. He gaped. *It isn't raining.*

In fact, outside, the weather was very nearly perfect. The
sky was still clear, the air smelled like pine pollen, and all of
Lem's history students were soaked. Mattie peeled off his jacket
and wrung it out, creating little puddles around his shoes. He
looked around for Lem, but Lem was nowhere to be found.

"What was that?" Eliot asked, eyes huge.

"A thunderstorm," Mattie panted, glancing at the other students to see if anyone else agreed, but everyone was too busy
being wet and miserable to pay attention to Mattie—who also

realized he was about to sound crazy. Or paranoid. Or crazily paranoid. "It was an *inside* thunderstorm."

The Spencers exchanged a look Mattie knew all too well. It said: *Something's very wrong here.* Although sometimes it also said: *We'd like another dessert.*

Caroline sat down on the bottom step and shook water out of her shoes and hair. She looked at Mattie like he was one of the Biology frogs she was always rescuing. "You must've hit your head when the Falcon crashed."

"And now you're hallucinating," Eliot added.

Mattie paused. Maybe the Spencers had a point. Maybe the Spencers had a great point, because inside thunderstorms *did* sound like something someone with a head injury would see. Except . . . "I know I saw wispy stuff on the ceiling. It looked like a cloud."

Caroline shook her head sadly. "Who's the president, Mattie?"

"I'm serious."

"What's two plus two?"

Mattie glared at her. "The ceiling was raining!" he hissed.

Caroline turned to her brother. "I got nothing."

"I'm telling you—"

Caroline held up one water-wrinkled hand, attention still pinned to Eliot. "You deal with him," she said and went back to drying off, muttering about boys and rain and how boys soaked with rain smelled like wet dogs.

Mattie blew out a long sigh. "Eliot, you gotta believe me."

"Ceilings don't rain."

"And headmasters don't clone students," Mattie whispered, leaning close. "This is *Munchem*."

Mattie paused, waiting for the reminder to sink in. He knew it did when Eliot's expression turned pained, like he was being forced to eat worms.

Or carpet tacks.

Eliot shrugged. "You probably just saw something that wasn't there."

"Again, this is Munchem." Mattie shook his head, spraying water like a Labrador. "All sorts of creepy stuff happens around here."

"Raining ceilings isn't really creepy. It's more . . ."

Mattie and Eliot went quiet as they tried to decide what raining ceilings were.

"Impractical?" Caroline finally volunteered, tugging one shoe back on.

Eliot nodded. "You probably saw dust or something and it set off the sprinkler system. They can repair Munchem all they want. It's still old."

Another good point, Mattie thought. Apparently Eliot was just full of them today. The sun beat down on Mattie, drying his clothes and making the soaked wool smell moldy. Maybe he *had* hit his head?

"What a day! How exciting!" Lem power walked past. His

white lab coat was now a dingy gray. It looked cold and heavy as it dribbled around his legs. "Guess they need to work on the fire sprinklers next, huh?"

See, Caroline mouthed to Mattie.

Mattie ignored her. He grabbed Lem's sleeve. "It wasn't the sprinkler system. You saw it too. There was some sort of cloud on the ceiling. It looked almost like fog, but it wasn't."

"Ha! You're funny, Mattie!" Lem said and then he laughed like it was the most hilarious idea ever, but there was something forced, something *false* behind the laugh and Mattie heard it.

In earlier years, he had heard the same false note when his mother told his father she'd "had this old dress for ages." In later years, he would hear the same false note when a certain politician swore he had "nothing in his pockets." There was something about lying that turned people's voices squeaky or distracted or vague and Mattie always noticed it.

Just like he was noticing it now.

Lem turned away to help two girls empty water out of their backpacks. Everyone was trying—and failing—to tidy up.

Mattie nudged Eliot. "Did Lem sound weird to you?"

Eliot paused from shaking water out of his ears. "What? No. He sounds like he always does."

"Are you sure?"

"Yeah. Positive."

"He doesn't seem off to you?"

"It's *Lem*." Eliot thought for a moment. "Maybe you should go see the nurse."

Mattie frowned. Maybe Eliot was right—not about the nurse, but about Lem. The scientist was always a little late, a little strange, and a lot, well, Lem. In other words, Lem being Lem was a perfectly good explanation.

Mattie turned his attention to his still-soaked jacket, but no matter how much he told himself Eliot was right, Mattie knew he wasn't. Lem was hiding something. Lem had *lied*.

The question was: why? Why wouldn't Lem admit there was more going on than a broken sprinkler system? It wasn't like the scientist had a problem talking about other failed experiments—and that's what this was, right? Some weird Larimore Corporation project?

Why not just say so?

Lem faced his students. "Class dismissed, everyone."

Cheers went up.

"We'll reconvene tomorrow. For those of you who don't know what that means, reconvene means we will meet again."

Less cheers. Lem didn't notice. He patted his coat pockets and pants pockets like he'd forgotten something and raced off toward the school gym.

Mattie nudged Eliot. "Want to go get changed?"

Eliot nodded and a very soggy Mattie led the equally soggy Spencers down the science wing's granite steps, through the stone arched arcade, and toward the once overgrown courtyard. Since class was still in session for everyone else, Munchem was oddly quiet. No one was running past them. No one was arguing. No one was trying to stuff anyone else under the bleachers. And *no one* was paying any attention to the shadow creeping through the school.

KNOW WHO YOU ARE

THE BOYS OF 14A LIVED ON THE SECOND FLOOR BEHIND A SINGLE red door. It wasn't the biggest dorm room (that one was next to the library) and it wasn't the smallest dorm room (that one was under the garden shed), but Mattie found it pretty comfortable, especially since the improvements.

The carpet was no longer dirt colored, the windows no longer shook when the wind blew, and the bunk beds no longer swayed . . . much. Unfortunately, the door still stuck and Mattie had to slam his shoulder into it twice before it popped opened. He fell into the room with Eliot right behind him.

Their roommate, Kent, was sitting on his bed. He looked up from his comic book and watched as Mattie and Eliot picked themselves up off the floor. "Hey, Eliot. Hey, Little Larimore."

"Hey, Kent." Mattie sighed. He'd been every dog name Carter could think of, New Kid, and now he was Little Larimore. Honestly, it was a bit disheartening. Mattie nudged Eliot and dropped his voice to whisper: "Why doesn't Carter ever get nicknames?"

"Because Carter doesn't answer to them." Eliot paused. "And because everyone knows what he did with that dead possum last semester."

"Why would that matter?"

"Would *you* want roadkill put in your bed?" Kent asked without looking up. "Because Carter would do it—and laugh about it. He doesn't believe in revenge being served cold or whatever. He likes it stinky and he likes to put it in the worst places."

This was true. Lots of stuff had changed between Mattie and his older brother, but this particular aspect of Carter's personality had not. He did enjoy a good practical joke, and he enjoyed revenge even more.

Eliot squished over to his bunk and sat down. "What are you doing here?" he asked Kent.

"What does it look like?" Their roommate turned another page of his comic. Mattie sat on his trunk and peeled off his wet socks. It looked like Kent was skipping class.

"Won't your teacher look for you up here?" Mattie asked, dropping both socks onto the floor.

"Nah." Kent turned another page. "Dr. Hoo has some

project he's working on. He's obsessed. Half the class is gone and he hasn't even noticed."

Mattie turned his attention to his wet pants and shirt. It did sound very, well, Dr. Hoo–like. Actually, it sounded like most of the new teachers. Mr. Larimore had moved all his scientists to Munchem to teach classes. It was a great idea until everyone realized the scientists didn't like the students and the students didn't like the scientists.

Well, except for Lem. Everyone loved Lem.

"Maybe you could pay Carter to make everyone stop calling you Little Larimore." Kent turned another page. "He can get anything done for the right price."

This was true. For ten dollars, Carter could get whatever candy you wanted. For twenty, he could get you answers to your homework—and for another five, they would be the *right* answers to your homework.

Mattie tugged on a clean, dry shirt. "I think I'll just tough it out."

"Suit yourself," Kent said, eyes never leaving his comic book.

Eliot tied the laces of his still-damp shoes and squelched to his feet. "Want to go watch the roofers swear at each other?" he asked Mattie.

Mattie nodded. "Kent?"

Kent still didn't look up. "Nah, I'm good."

Eliot and Mattie slammed 14A's door behind them, but

because it was 14A's door they had to slam it twice more before it closed. Mattie trotted down the stairs and Eliot followed him.

"Maybe you should hit Doyle with a dirty sponge again," Eliot said, jumping the last two steps to land next to Mattie. "It certainly made an impression on him."

Mattie frowned. He had indeed hit Doyle with a dirty sponge. On impulse and *after* Doyle had hawked a loogie on him. As a general practice, Mattie didn't hit people—with sponges or anything else—but the reminder took him back to that day, and Mattie was so busy thinking about it, he didn't notice the small blond girl standing in Munchem's foyer until Eliot elbowed him.

"New kid," Eliot whispered. The new kid was odd looking. She wore a small navy business suit and she carried a small silver briefcase. Her hair was slicked into a knot so tight that it seemed to lift her eyebrows into a permanent expression of *Huh?*

Mattie slowed.

"What are you doing?" Eliot elbowed him. "C'mon."

But Mattie couldn't. He remembered what being the new kid was like. Until Mattie learned his way around, Munchem's vines looked poisonous and its stone angels looked murderous. Until he met the Spencers, the other students didn't look friendly. They looked like they wanted to push him down. Actually, that part was accurate. The other students still wanted to push him down.

Bottom line, Mattie knew Munchem could be awfully intimidating at first, so he gave the blond girl a big, welcoming smile. "Hello. Are you lost?"

The girl turned to them and sniffed. "I'm never lost. I'm looking for Mathias Littleton Larimore."

"Oh." Mattie hesitated, suddenly very, very aware that the blond girl was studying every inch of him and she did *not* look impressed. In fact, she looked like she was more than a little disgusted. "Uh, that's me," Mattie said at last.

The girl's eyes narrowed. "Well, I'm Delia Dane and I'm your archnemesis."

TRUST YOUR INSTINCTS

I'M KIDDING. DELIA DIDN'T INTRODUCE HERSELF LIKE THAT—ALTHOUGH it would've been easier on everyone if she had. But that's true for most people, not just archenemies. If your neighbor would just *say* that he doesn't appreciate you watering your lawn in your underwear instead of covering your yard in pink plastic flamingos, life would be easier. Just like life would have been easier for Mattie if Delia had just said, "One day, I'm going to dangle you over a vat of acid and laugh about it."

But she didn't. In reality, Delia said: "Well, I'm Delia Dane and I'm stuck here because of *you*."

Mattie blinked and then blinked some more. He had no idea what to say to that. He looked at Eliot. Eliot was also blinking. He had no idea what to say either. In some ways, telling a person she's stuck at Munchem because of you is just as alarming as telling someone you are his archnemesis.

Okay, maybe not, but *nothing* is as alarming as being dangled over a vat of acid. Trust me on this.

Mattie turned back to Delia. "Uh, *what*?" he finally managed.

"You heard me," Delia said brightly. She hugged her silver briefcase to her chest as if it were her favorite teddy bear. "I'm stuck here because of you. It's your fault and I'm going to make you pay for it."

Eliot shouldered Mattie to the side. "Why would it be Mattie's fault—"

"Oh! Delia! There you are!" Professor Shelley rushed down the hallway, tugging her black cardigan around her thin frame. "You mustn't wander off. We still need to get your class schedule."

"I have it." Delia brandished a single piece of paper in her fist. It looked especially white in the sunlight streaming through the windows. That was something else Eliot and Mattie would eventually learn about Delia: she always looked pristine and polished. It was part of her disguise. No one ever suspects the preppy girl.

But where were we? Oh, yes. Professor Shelley was confused. She cocked her head. "How did you get your sched— Never mind. This is Mattie Larimore and Eliot Spencer. They'll be in most of your classes." The professor paused, eyes narrowing. She looked from Mattie to Eliot and back again. "Boys, why is your hair wet?"

"The sprinkler system malfunctioned in Professor Lem's class." Eliot's grin was wide as his face, maybe even wider. "Water went *everywhere*."

"The sprinkler system malfunction—*oh!*" Professor Shelley's mouth rounded, and she glanced at Delia. "I have to go. Mattie?"

"Yes?"

"Show Delia around."

"I—"

It was no good though. Professor Shelley was already running the other way. She dashed down the corridor, black cardigan flapping like bat wings.

Eliot watched her go and sighed happily. "She always appreciates how informed I am."

Mattie highly doubted this, but he was too busy being stared down by Delia to say so. "Why is it my fault you're at Munchem?" he asked at last.

Delia narrowed her eyes, and said nothing.

Ooooookay, Mattie thought.

"Are you a bad kid?" Eliot asked. "Because that's really the only reason anyone comes to Munchem."

Somehow Delia managed to narrow her eyes even more. It was rather terrifying, and Mattie didn't know if that was an agreement or a denial. He also didn't know how he was supposed to show Delia around when clearly Delia was only interested in hating him. But his dad always said Mattie should fake it until he made it, so . . .

"So this is the foyer," Mattie said, gesturing to the sloped ceiling and the worn stone floor.

Delia raised one brow. "Are we *really* going to do this? I know my way around."

"How? You just got here."

"I have my ways."

Again, Mattie had nothing to say to that. Thankfully though he didn't have to, because at that moment Caroline pushed through the front doors, sodden ponytail snapping like a whip.

"Hey," she said.

"Hey," Mattie and Eliot returned.

"Professor Shelley asked me to meet her here. Something about the new kid." Caroline glanced at Delia. "I'm guessing that's you?"

Delia arched an eyebrow. "*You're* supposed to be my new friend?"

"If you're lucky," Caroline said.

Delia's eyebrow arched higher. "I don't like your tone."

Everyone paused, and as Mattie watched, Caroline's expression darkened. This isn't going to end well, Mattie thought.

And he was right.

"Well, I don't like your . . ." Caroline looked up and down Delia, and frowned. "I don't like your face."

"I'm going to give you precisely two seconds to apologize for that."

Caroline looked precisely two seconds away from pummeling Delia into a smear on the floor. "I'm sorry I don't like your face?" she ventured.

Mattie grabbed Caroline's arm. "Okay, well, uh," he said to Delia. "Glad you know your way around. We'll see you later then."

"Oh, you'll be seeing me," Delia said, and she leaned very, *very* close to Mattie. "I'm going to take you down, Larimore," she whispered.

Well, yay for me, Mattie thought as he watched Delia stalk down the hallway. The hairs on the back of Mattie's neck stood up and his teeth itched, but he was too stunned to notice.

"That was really weird," Eliot said. "Why's it your fault she's here?"

Mattie shrugged. "I've never met her!"

"Huh," Caroline said. "She certainly doesn't like you."

Mattie rolled his eyes. "Like you made such a good impression."

The loudspeaker crackled with an announcement and Mattie shook his head. He still had water in his ears and it turned the announcement into a dull *wah wah wah*.

"What was that?" Mattie asked the Spencers, sticking one finger in his ear. It didn't do any good. The water just sloshed around. "What'd Rooney say?"

"Everyone has to go to their dorms," Eliot said. Caroline's ponytail was still dripping everywhere and Eliot took a moment to smear the water around on the hardwood floor. "The new school sprinkler systems are malfunctioning."

Considering Mattie's hair was still damp, this was hardly a revelation. He sighed. "Great. Now I can spend all afternoon worrying about why the new girl wants to take me down." Mattie paused, noticing again how his skin was prickling and his teeth were itching.

She's going to be a problem, said the voice inside Mattie's head. It was a very small voice, but it usually had good ideas. Except for the time it suggested Mattie steal a subway train.

"I have a bad feeling about Delia," Mattie said.

Caroline tossed her ponytail again. "It's not like she can actually *do* anything to you."

Mattie nodded. Caroline was always right, but in this case we know she's wrong, and we know things at Munchem are about to get much, much worse.

LANDSLIDES, PIRATES, DETENTION: THERE ARE LOADS OF THINGS THAT CAN TAKE DOWN YOUR TEAM. BE PREPARED.

THINGS DIDN'T GET WORSE FOR MATTIE RIGHT AWAY THOUGH. IN fact, dinner and evening study hall were downright boring and Delia didn't look in Mattie's direction even once. Caroline took this as a sign she was right again.

"Say it," she said to Mattie as they sat in Professor Shelley's class the next morning. The hallway and classrooms smelled like fresh baked bread today. It was way better than pumpkin pies that smelled like hamster cages, but it also made Mattie hungry.

"Say it," Caroline repeated.

Mattie sighed. "You were right."

She grinned.

"Stop telling her when she's right," Eliot said, not taking

his eyes away from his computer screen. "It makes her insufferable." He thought for a moment. "More insufferable."

"Quiet!" Professor Shelley shoved away from her desk with such force, the sole picture of her daughter wobbled. She paced to the server bank, long feet slapping the tile like a scuba diver walking to water. "I'm trying to work here!"

Everyone fell quiet.

Or they did until Professor Shelley rushed into the hallway, heading somewhere else. Technically, she wasn't supposed to leave her students, but the scientists seemed to have difficulty grasping what teachers were supposed to do, and apparently this was one of those times.

Mattie thumped his pencil against his desktop and watched Maxwell and Doyle began to smack each other. Smacking quickly escalated into thumping and thumping turned into wrestling. The boys crashed into Delia's desk and she glared at them, face pale with rage.

Mattie shuddered. "Delia's rooming with you, right?" he whispered to Caroline.

"Yeah." Caroline's belly churned as Beezus curled up for his midmorning nap. "She's weird. She said she was giving me one last chance to be her friend."

Mattie blinked. That *was* weird—and a little disturbing. "What did you say?"

"That she was being weird. Honestly, I think her hair's pulled a little too tight." Beezus squeaked and Caroline petted him through her sweater. "There, there," she said to him. The rat trembled. Mattie couldn't tell if it was because Beezus was always trembling or if he was cold.

Personally, Mattie was freezing. Professor Shelley's classroom was always too bright and too cold because their Computer Science professor was a worrier. She worried the servers would overheat. She worried the students would spill things. She did not actually worry about her students though, and two months into the new semester, Mattie was getting used to seeing his breath rise in hazy puffs as he worked.

Or when he was supposed to be working. Eliot had pretty much taken over their project. They were supposed to troubleshoot and fix various computer programs for the scientists working in the gym. Eliot liked to call it "bringing them back to life." Mattie and Caroline liked to call it "boring."

"Okay," Eliot said, looking up from their latest string of broken code. "Write down that the whole program crashes when you enter zeroes into the left-hand field."

Dutifully, Mattie wrote it down, or at least, he did until his pencil tip snapped halfway through.

"Here." Caroline leaned down and took a pencil box out of her bag. "You gotta be prepared." The pencil box's lid bent back and a dozen roaches leaped out. They surged up Caroline's hands. They ran across her forearms. They leaped for her face.

"Eeek!" Caroline screamed.

"Wha—?" Eliot glanced up and got a roach in the face. He flailed. "Oh gross!"

The roach went flying and Mattie ducked as it sailed past him. *Whap!* It hit another student's desk.

"Nasty!" That student swept the roach onto someone else.

"Ack!" Everyone jumped up, as Professor Shelley dashed back through the door.

"Students!" she screamed. "Students!"

The students ignored her. They ran around, they hopped on desks, and, in the case of Doyle and Maxwell, they stomped roaches.

Not that Mattie noticed any of that. He bent down and scooped up the pencil box. It was empty—or was it? Mattie peered closer. There was a small note taped to the box's bottom. It said:

YOU WERE WARNED.

Unfortunately for Caroline, roaches were only the beginning. When she went to the bathroom, Delia stole all the toilet paper. When she went to sleep, Delia used the stolen toilet paper to roll Caroline to her bed, and when Caroline ate lunch, Delia swapped her vegetarian meatballs for real meatballs and Caroline threw up until her eyes watered.

So it was rather understandable that by the time Caroline staggered into Professor Shelley's class on Friday, there was a wild look in Beezus's eyes and dark shadows under Caroline's.

Mattie scooted over so she could join him on their workbench. "You have to tell one of the teachers. This is wrong!"

Caroline put her head down on the desk. "I'd have to prove it first and I can't. My roommates are helping her."

Mattie's mouth hung open. *"Why?"*

"Because they're afraid she'll do the same thing to them." Caroline sat up and rubbed a hand across her face.

"I can't do it." Eliot shoved back from the keyboard, and scowled at the line of green code across their computer screen. "It's impossible."

"Excuse me," Caroline said, eyes slit in anger. "But I'm having a crisis at the moment. Do you think you could pay attention?"

"Sorry," Eliot said, "but it really is impossible."

"Maybe for you it is."

Mattie and the Spencers stiffened, turned, and saw Delia Dane standing behind them. Her blond hair was tied up in a knot again. Or still. Mattie wasn't sure.

"Oh, yeah?" Eliot crossed his arms. "Well, if you're so special, you fix it."

"I will. Move."

Eliot moved. They all watched in silence as Delia worked. Her fingers flew even faster than Eliot's.

"There," she said, stepping back. "Done."

"No way." Eliot sounded disgusted. He leaned forward to inspect the code and his jaw dropped. "No. Way."

Mattie felt unease tiptoe down his spine. Eliot didn't sound disgusted anymore. He sounded in awe.

"You're *fast*," Eliot said, scrolling through the code.

"Of course, I am," Delia said, flicking lint from her sweater onto Caroline.

Eliot looked up. "Would you teach me?"

"Maybe." Delia tossed her hair. Or tried to toss her hair. With any other girl, this would make their braids or ponytails or loose hair bounce, but as far as Mattie could tell, Delia's hair never bounced. It stayed in its tight knot as if glued with cement. She strolled off like the world was watching, which it wasn't, but Eliot certainly was.

Caroline looked down at her paper, gripping her pen hard enough to shake. "I can't believe I have to share a dorm with her. She's making Beezus molt. He's been a nervous wreck since she moved in."

Mattie eyed Caroline's stomach, picturing the rat that was curled behind her sweater. There were a lot of things that made Beezus molt—things like allergies and unpeeled grapes and days that ended in *Y* being at the top of the list.

Mattie glanced at Eliot expecting to see his friend nodding in agreement. But Eliot wasn't nodding or agreeing. He stared into the distance, looking a bit ill.

"Are you about to be sick?" Mattie asked. In truth, Mattie didn't think Eliot looked sick so much as weird. His friend's eyes were glassy and his mouth was slightly open. Eliot panted ever so slightly.

Okay, he looked sick *and* weird, but the important thing to remember here is Mattie and Caroline had no idea why.

But I do, because the "worse" I promised you had arrived in another horrible wave. Eliot Spencer had just fallen in love with Delia Dane.

EVERYONE HAS A WEAKNESS

"SHE'S MAGNIFICENT," ELIOT SAID SOFTLY, EYES STILL GLASSY.

Mattie gaped. "What?"

"Delia." Eliot sat back in his chair and passed one hand over his face. "She's magnificent. How could I not have seen it before?"

Mattie looked at Caroline and Caroline looked at Mattie. They both swallowed. Eliot watched Delia as if she were made of magic. Mattie peered closely at the girl, trying to see what Eliot saw, and failed.

Although Mattie did appreciate how she could throw an elbow. Delia managed to hit Doyle right in the softest spot on his side. The bigger boy yelped and looked around. When he saw Delia walking away, his eyes narrowed, but he didn't follow her. Delia just didn't look like the kind of girl who would elbow someone.

"You can't possibly like her," Caroline said at last, nose wrinkled. "She's *horrible*."

"So is everyone here." Eliot paused. "Well, everyone except for Mattie. He's the only good kid."

"Sometimes that's debatable," Mattie reminded him.

"True."

"Hey!" Caroline snapped her fingers and her brother blinked. "Focus. She's horrible to me. How could you like her?"

Eliot's eyes went wide. "How could I *not*? We have the same interests, the same taste!"

"It's the computer stuff," Mattie told Caroline, feeling a touch relieved. It couldn't possibly be serious if Eliot just liked Delia for her computer skills.

"Of course it's her computer skills!" Eliot rubbed one hand over his heart as if it were threatening to escape his chest. "I'm telling you, she's perfect."

"She's a perfect pain," Caroline muttered.

Mattie agreed. This was going to be a problem.

Still there are worse reasons to like someone—falling for someone's money or looks or what they can do for you being at the top of the list. But Eliot wasn't thinking of anything like that. He fell for Delia's skills and intelligence, which are excellent reasons to fall in love with someone.

Except in this case. Because eventually Delia would use

those skills and that intelligence in a never-ending quest for world domination. Then again, some people enjoy ambition in their spouses.

The electronic bell rang and all the students began to push for the door, voices rising in an unintelligible rumble. Mattie threw his supplies into his book bag, and when he looked up, he spotted Delia pushing through the other students. She reached Eliot, and he grinned.

"If you really want to learn how to do that, I'll show you." Delia flicked her eyes over Mattie and Caroline. "But only you," she said, and brushed past them.

Delia disappeared into the crowded hallway and Eliot heaved an enormous sigh. His smile was gummy. "I've never wanted anything more."

They were strong words, and Mattie would've been amazed except Eliot had used the same expression to describe his computer's hard-drive upgrade.

This will pass, Mattie thought, slinging his backpack over one shoulder. *It has to.*

Behind Eliot, Caroline mimed vomiting and Mattie laughed.

"What?" Eliot asked.

"Nothing," Mattie told him. Out in the hallway, the scent of strawberries had now joined the fresh baked bread and Mattie's stomach growled. Lunch could not come soon enough. Caroline's sweater rolled as Beezus turned in happy circles. Apparently, the rat agreed.

"Hey! Hey, Mattie!" Carter shouldered a couple of seventh graders out of his way and headed toward them. There were red sweater marks on his face as if he'd been sleeping on his arm and his shirt was untucked. "Dad wants to see us," Carter said.

Mattie's chest squeezed. "Are we in trouble?"

"Aren't we always?"

"No, usually that's just you."

Carter smiled bashfully. "Oh, shucks, Mattie, you say the nicest things."

Mattie turned to go with his brother. "I'll see you guys later," he said to the Spencers.

"Good luck," Caroline said.

"Magnificent," Eliot added.

It would've been confusing if Eliot hadn't still been staring after Delia. Actually, no, it was still confusing. Carter stared at Eliot like he had something growing out of his ear. "What's magnificent?" Carter asked.

"Long story," Mattie told him. "Let's go."

KNOW WHEN TO BUY

THE WINDOW-LINED HALLWAY THAT LED TO THE HEADMASTER'S office was brighter and cleaner than ever. Bars of sunlight streamed through the windows, turning the polished floorboards silvery and the polished wood trim glossy. Recent dusting even made the headmasters' portraits look cheerful. Okay, *fine*, it didn't, but I'm not sure anything could make Olga Higgins appear cheerful.

Mattie kept his head down to avoid looking at her, but it didn't really matter. The headmistress's painted, squinty eyes bored holes into the back of his head.

"I hate these things," Carter said as they neared Headmaster Rooney's office. It wasn't exactly a shocking revelation. Carter always hated meeting with their dad. Mattie knew this because of the way his brother always scowled, and also because Carter always said so. "It's like he just wants to hear himself talk," his brother continued.

Mattie had to admit Carter had a point. "Maybe this time it will be better?"

"You're such a Susie Sunshine, you know that—"

"Carter! Mattie!" Headmaster Rooney came flying around the corner. He raced toward the boys with long strides, his red hair shimmering under the lights. "Good to see you boys! It's been a while!"

"Yeah, like since breakfast," Carter said.

"Exactly!" The headmaster was all smiles. "Your father is a genius!" He clapped one hand to his heart as if it were fluttering. "A genius!"

"Oh, yeah?" Carter looked unconvinced. "Why's that?"

"One word for you." The Rooster leaned close and Mattie could see even his nose hairs were red. "Students as publicity!"

"That's three words," Carter said.

"But one message!"

Carter nodded like he understood and it made Headmaster Rooney smile even wider.

"I don't get it," Mattie said.

"Oh, you will! C'mon! C'mon!" The Rooster raced ahead of them, his shiny shoes slapping against the floorboards.

Carter looked at Mattie. "Still think this is going to be better? There's a 'message.'"

Mattie had to admit it did sound like the meeting wasn't going to be better, and once he walked into the headmaster's office, he *knew* it wasn't going to be better. Mr. Larimore was standing at the cluttered headmaster's desk with employees crowded around him. Two of the employees were chewing their fingernails. One was swaying and muttering to himself, and one was shouting.

I've never seen Dr. Hoo so mad, Mattie thought.

"I've never been so mad!" Dr. Hoo shouted.

"Now, now," Mr. Larimore said. The short, round scientist actually looked tall next to Mattie's dad. "Don't be like that, Dr. Hoo. This is just a temporary setback."

Dr. Hoo stuck both fists in the pockets of his white lab coat. "No one appreciates me around here. I haven't had a raise in"—Dr. Hoo stared at the ceiling as he thought—"forever."

"Dr. Hoo." Mr. Larimore put one hand on Dr. Hoo's shoulder. "Here at Larimore Corporation, we value you in ways that can't be expressed with money."

Dr. Hoo's mouth went thin as a paper cut.

Mr. Larimore shuffled some black plastic boxes on his desk, and spotted Carter and Mattie standing in the doorway. "Boys! Glad you could make it!"

"Did we have a choice?" Carter asked.

"Oh, son." Mr. Larimore smiled and shook his head as if Carter were an adorable puppy instead of an almost fourteen-year-old boy. "You always make me laugh."

Except Mr. Larimore wasn't laughing. His eyes had gone glinty, and it made Carter grin.

Mr. Larimore pointed to the last two empty seats. "Make yourselves comfortable. We're almost finished."

Mattie suppressed a groan as Dr. Hoo stalked out the door. Mattie wished he could go with him. For grown-ups, "almost finished" could mean they were in fact almost finished, but it could also mean they were nowhere near finished and Mattie would have to sit there until he died. When it came to Mr. Larimore, the boys never knew which it would be.

Mattie dropped into the closest chair. Surprisingly, Headmaster Rooney's office still looked the same: heavy, dark furniture, lots of pictures of Headmaster Rooney hugging famous people, and, presumably, a closet still filled with coats that still hid a door that still led to a basement that still housed a cloning machine.

Mattie swung his legs back and forth. Eliot was right. It was rather nice some things stayed the same. And Mattie tried to concentrate on that as he waited and waited until the other Larimore corporation employees left and Mr. Larimore finally turned back to his sons.

"Now! Boys!" Mr. Larimore said with his toothiest grin. "I've called you in today so we can discuss the next step in Munchem's evolution!"

Mr. Larimore seemed to have forgotten he was in the

headmaster's office and not on a stage. Mattie had to resist covering his ears against his father's bellowing.

"We're going to make the Larimore Corporation even better!" Mr. Larimore continued while Mattie sneaked a look at his brother. Carter's face was carefully blank, but Mattie could see a single thought churning through his brother's brain: What did Munchem have to do with making Larimore Corporation better?

"So! With greatness in mind! I bring you . . ." Mr. Larimore held up a newspaper. The front page had a huge picture of Mr. Larimore and Rooney holding shovels and pretending to dig a hole. "Larimore Corporation giving back!"

Headmaster Rooney clapped. "One message!"

Mattie and Carter stared at the newspaper. Mattie blinked. He blinked again.

"I know what you're thinking," Mr. Larimore said.

"I really hope not," Carter whispered.

"You're thinking this is genius! This is brilliant!" Mr. Larimore's eyes were bright, bright, *bright*. He rubbed his hands together. "This is my best idea yet, isn't it?"

"It's great, Dad." Out of the corner of his eye, Mattie saw Carter turn toward him and stare. Mattie forced his smile wider. Their dad was really trying, so Mattie figured he'd try too. "But, uh, what exactly is 'Larimore Corporation giving back'?"

"I'm so glad you asked, Mattie!" Mr. Larimore dropped into one of the headmaster's plushy chairs and scooted it closer to his sons. Next to him, Headmaster Rooney vibrated with excitement. "You see, boys, Larimore Corporation has had a few, ah, unfortunate setbacks."

"What are setbacks?" Mattie asked.

"Screwups," Carter said.

Mr. Larimore threw his oldest son a dark look. "Not what I would call them, but yes, screwups. There was a little issue with blue pizza dough and now the Aluminum Falcon isn't performing to expectations. The public doesn't think the Larimore Corporation is on top of its game—that's where the new publicity plan will come into play. People love adorable children, cats doing funny things, and carbs." Mr. Larimore paused, staring into the distance. His mustache twitched. "Maybe I should consider having a cat ride the Aluminum Falcon next," he muttered.

Carter rolled his eyes. "I still don't get how this is going to help anyone."

Mr. Larimore settled both hands on top of his round belly. "I've invested heavily into Munchem—I mean, that new ventilation system was not cheap, let me tell you—and that ballroom I turned into a gym! Do you know how much better it looks now? Do you know how *expensive* that was?"

Mattie didn't. None of the students was allowed in the ballroom turned into a gym because the gym had recently been turned into a laboratory for the scientists. "Actually," Mattie said, "it's off-limits—"

But Mr. Larimore didn't stop: "I *knew* taking over Munchem would be expensive. I also knew Munchem could get me something money can't buy."

"What's that?" Mattie asked.

"Good publicity." Mr. Larimore steepled his fingers and studied the black plastic boxes on his desk. Now that Mattie was closer, he could see they weren't boxes at all. They were security cameras. What was his dad doing with them?

"You see, boys," Mr. Larimore continued, "Larimore Corporation giving back is all about the company making improvements on the school and the students doing good works for the community."

"And letting everyone know you do them," Carter added, swiping the newspaper off Rooney's desk to study the picture.

"Precisely!" Mr. Larimore grinned and grinned. "If you don't tell everyone what a good person you are, how will they know? In this case, if we don't tell everyone how much Larimore Corporation is doing for children, how will they know?"

Suspicion, small and hard and round, rolled through Mattie's stomach. "So how is it going to work?"

"Well," Mr. Larimore said, patting his shiny, bald head, "in this case, we're going to do a photo shoot with Ambassador Theodore Wade—he's said some unfortunate things about the company and we're going to show him what the Larimore Corporation is truly capable of."

"By doing what?" Mattie asked. "Standing around and smiling gratefully for the camera?"

Mr. Larimore beamed. "Now you're getting it!"

Actually, Mattie wasn't so sure he was. "And the security cameras?"

"Oh. Those." Mr. Larimore frowned, flicking the closest security camera with a finger. "Dr. Shelley is going to pull all the cameras so we can do an upgrade. Can't be too careful. Did you know hackers can use our own cameras to spy on us? She told me all about it."

Mattie paused, thinking about Eliot, and Eliot's computer, Marilyn, and how he could absolutely believe Eliot would use Marilyn to spy on someone. "No," he said at last. "I didn't."

"It's true," Mr. Larimore said, snatching the newspaper back from Carter. "Shelley's right: our competition will stop at nothing to steal our technology. That's what happens when you're the best. I had to protect us. First, we'll do the perimeter cameras. Then we'll do the cameras at the gym. She has a plan."

"Yippee for Professor Shelley," Carter muttered, sliding lower in his chair.

Mr. Larimore's mustache twitched as he glared at his son. "*Anyway*, I'm going to need both of you to help me. I need you to be excited! Thrilled! About this new opportunity!"

Mattie thought their dad sounded thrilled enough for all of them, and judging by Carter's expression, his brother agreed. Mr. Larimore sat back, eyes on the Rooster, who was smiling again.

"This is my favorite part of business," Mr. Larimore told the headmaster. "I love thinking outside the box."

"But what if it doesn't work?" Mattie asked.

"Oh." Mr. Larimore took a security camera and spun it against the desktop. "I'm prepared for that. Not all plans work out. The important thing is to know when to quit."

"Which means?" Carter asked.

"Larimore Corporation will withdraw funding and Munchem will close."

FOCUS ON THE POSITIVE

MUNCHEM WOULD CLOSE? IT WAS NOT A PLEASANT DISCOVERY, and every time Mattie thought of it, his stomach squeezed. Mattie sat in his chair for a long moment.

I'm going to have to save the school, he thought. *Again*.

"Great, isn't it?" Headmaster Rooney swung his legs back and forth, his grin blank as ever.

"Now," Mr. Larimore said, sweeping up from his chair. "I'm going to need your help. Tell all your little friends how exciting it is to meet Ambassador Wade. We want everyone thrilled at the opportunity!"

"I can't tell anyone." His brother crossed his arms and looked at their dad. "I don't have any friends," he lied.

Mr. Larimore's mustache twitched twice. "With an attitude like yours, I believe it."

Carter scowled. Mr. Larimore scowled. Mattie wilted. His mom and dad always believed the worst about Carter. They didn't know him like Mattie knew him. Of course, that also meant they didn't know about the time Carter tied Mattie up and hung from his closet rod. It had been a very long and boring four hours.

Mr. Larimore's phone rang and he turned to answer it. Mattie waited for a moment, listening to his dad shout at whoever was on the other end. Words like "idiot" and "moron" and "he did *what*?" were being thrown around.

Mattie sighed. It sounded like Mr. Larimore was going to go on for a while.

"C'mon," Carter muttered, tugging Mattie toward the door. For several moments, the boys walked along in silence, but when they neared the cafeteria, Mattie couldn't be silent any longer.

"Do you think this will work?" he asked Carter.

"Of course not!"

"So what do we do?"

"Start looking for new schools."

"That wasn't what I meant." But it was too late. Carter banged through the cafeteria's double doors and joined his friends. Over at their usual table, the Spencers waved.

"How'd it go with your dad?" Eliot asked as Mattie sat down.

"Not good." Mattie stared at Caroline. She was scrubbing at her face so hard Beezus squeaked inside her sweater. "Are you okay?"

Caroline dropped her hands, revealing squiggly black marks under her nose. "What do you think?"

Mattie leaned in for a closer look. "That someone tried to draw a mustache on you and you woke up."

"Exactly." Caroline dipped her napkin in her water cup and went back to scrubbing. "So what's up with your dad? I saw Professor Shelley pulling down security cameras. She looked even more annoyed than usual."

Mattie nodded. "She said they're vulnerable to hackers or something. My dad's having her take them down."

"Is that what he wanted to talk to you about?" Eliot asked.

"Not really," Mattie said. "He's using Munchem for good publicity, and if he doesn't get enough good publicity, he's going to close the school."

"I don't understand," Caroline said as Beezus clawed her collar. Mattie tried to pay attention, but the mustache and rat kept distracting him. "How are we supposed to get him good publicity?"

Mattie quickly explained Ambassador Wade and the photo shoot and how Munchem was supposed to give his dad something money couldn't buy. With every word, Caroline's eyes grew wider and rounder.

"Getting out of class to do some stupid photo?" Eliot asked. "I'm game! This is the best idea your dad has ever had."

"He thinks so too," Mattie said.

Caroline shook her head. "It's a terrible idea!"

Her brother rolled his eyes. "Well, you're the only one who thinks so."

"No, I'm not!"

"Yes, you are!" Eliot pointed to Mattie. "Mattie thinks it's a great idea."

Mattie wasn't sure he would go that far, but he also wasn't so sure it mattered because the Spencers were already arguing. Or they were until Delia strolled by. She had three girls from seventh grade following her and even though she didn't even *glance* at Eliot, he snapped up straight and ran one hand over his hair.

"I can't believe you like her!" Caroline whispered furiously. "Look what she did to me!"

Frankly, it was hard *not* to look at what Delia did to Caroline. Mattie's eyes kept straying to the black marks.

Eliot rounded on his sister. "Well, maybe if you tried a little harder!"

Caroline gaped. "Why do I have to try harder?"

"Because you don't have any friends other than us! You don't always have to hang out with me!"

Caroline gaped. "Forget it!" She jumped up and stomped off.

Eliot glared at his sister's back. "Whatever," he said, turning to Mattie. "It's not like I need her anyway."

Mattie picked at the tabletop, and watched Eliot watch Delia. It made Mattie lose his appetite. Mr. Larimore's favorite part of Munchem might be the business opportunities, but Mattie's favorite part was his friends, and if they weren't friends anymore, well, what was left?

WATCH WHERE YOU'RE GOING

A WEEK LATER, CAROLINE STILL WASN'T SPEAKING TO MATTIE or Eliot. She didn't sit with them during class and she didn't sit with them during meals. Eliot said he didn't care and maybe it was true, but Mattie did care. A lot.

Especially at the moment, because he (along with the rest of the Munchem sixth grade) was standing in the hot sun while a photographer tried to make the students look very happy about meeting Ambassador Wade. It was strangely warm for April, and Mattie was sweaty, tired, and pretty sure Caroline would've had something funny to say about the whole thing.

"Again!" Mr. Larimore yelled at the photographer. Even though they'd been taking pictures for an hour, Mr. Larimore still wasn't happy. Mattie's dad stood behind the weedy photographer and glared at everyone. His big blue vein began to pulse.

"Smile!" Ambassador Wade said, wrapping one arm around Doyle's shoulders.

Doyle screamed and fell to the ground "It hurts! It hurts!"

Mattie sighed. There was no way the ambassador's grip had hurt Doyle, but it didn't matter. Everyone began to mill around, trying to see Doyle thrashing on the grass.

"We're never getting out of here," Mattie told Eliot. A few feet away from them, an oblivious Headmaster Rooney practiced different smiles. All of them looked pretty vacant.

Mr. Larimore hauled Doyle to his feet and shoved him back into place. "Try it again!" he shouted. "Smile like you mean it!"

"My arm!" Doyle shrieked and fell down again.

"Arm?" Headmaster Rooney sprang to attention. "Whose arm?" He tried to push through the students to see better, but the students pushed back.

"What kind of school is this?" Delia's voice rose above the crowd, and even though Mattie couldn't see her, he could somehow hear how she was pointing an imperious finger at Doyle. "Someone needs to get him a doctor! This is cruel!"

"Now I'm just getting bored." Mattie squinted up at the sun and tugged at his sweat-dampened shirt. It really was oddly hot. "I wish Caroline would come stand with us."

"I don't. I—" Eliot paused. "Do you hear that?"

"Hear what?" Mattie asked. "My will to live leaving me? Why, yes I do."

"No, like . . ." Eliot trailed off, looking toward the school gym. "Like *rumbling*."

"Do you have sunstroke or something?" Mattie turned to Eliot, and as he did, a cool wind snaked past, dragging thunder with it.

BOOM! The thunder rolled overhead as the wind began to gust. Deep purple clouds appeared above the gym's crumbling chimneys, moving quickly across the water-stained rooftop.

Moving straight for us, Mattie thought, just before the rumbling turned into rain, and the clouds swallowed the sun.

"Blast!" Mr. Larimore bellowed. "Run for the school!"

And for once, the students listened. Everyone took off as rain pelted down, stinging their faces and heads. Now, at other schools, the lawns would not be very big and the students would not have very far to run and the grass wouldn't turn to mud because bulldozers had been improving the school. But it wasn't any other school, it was Munchem, and it was bad.

And as Mattie dashed toward Munchem's sweeping granite steps, it got worse. The rain came down harder and the mud grew thicker and the ground began to crack and slide. A deep, *deep* jagged ravine snaked across the lawn.

"Aiiieee!" everyone screamed. The ground heaved again, and everyone ran faster. Eliot and Mattie raced toward the school. Caroline raced toward the parking lot. Delia tripped and fell

down. And the rest of Mattie's roommates? Well, Doyle made it out, but Kent and Bell were swallowed right up.

Munchem's lawn was no longer a lawn. It was a wide patch of raw dirt-and-rock-filled holes and a huge, raging ravine.

Actually, put like that, the no-longer-lawn was rather appropriate for Munchem, but Mattie didn't see it that way. The teachers had herded most of the students onto the front steps to wait for the school nurse.

"How many Munchem teachers does it take to get Kent and Bell out of a hole?" Delia asked as EMTs and Munchem scientists tried to pull Kent and Bell to safety. "Because it seems like this is math we could actually use around here."

Mattie slumped lower. He couldn't bring himself to argue. Kent and Bell had almost been *killed*.

So much for good publicity, Mattie thought. Ambassador Wade had peeled off in his sleek limousine, leaving Mr. Larimore standing in the now squishy driveway. Mattie had expected his dad to start yelling, but he hadn't. He had, however, gone stalking into the school like he was *going* to start yelling.

"How did this even happen?" Mattie whispered.

"I don't know." Eliot flicked a bit of grass in Caroline's

direction. "Erosion? I mean, they have been pushing a lot of dirt around. The ground's weak."

"And that thunderstorm was freaky strong."

Eliot frowned. "Yeah," he said at last.

"The storm came over the top of the gym—like it was coming *from* the gym." Standing on the steps, Mattie couldn't see the newly repaired ballroom turned gym, but he could glimpse the crouching gargoyles. The students weren't allowed inside, and frankly, Mattie wasn't feeling the loss. Maybe it was the spidery-armed candelabras that still glowed in the cloudy windows. Or maybe it was the near-constant smell of burned plastic. Probably it was the occasional scream coming from inside. But there was something disturbing about the once-upon-a-time ballroom.

"Are you worried?" Mattie asked at last.

Eliot thought for a moment. "Not at all."

Mattie could tell he was lying.

NEVER UNDERESTIMATE YOUR ENEMY

IT WAS ALMOST AS BAD AS WHEN MATTIE NEARLY DIED IN A diaper. For the next two weeks, all the students could talk about was mud and holes and how Kent and Bell could have *died*.

"I heard they're still in the hospital," one kid said as he passed Mattie during lunch.

"My parents are going to freak out," another kid added. "I bet they pull me out. This school is a disaster!"

Mattie pushed food around on his plate and watched Caroline push food around on her plate. She sat at the end of a bench, the girls from her dorm sitting next to her. But they weren't *with* her. In fact, as far as Mattie could tell, everyone was ignoring Caroline and Caroline was ignoring everyone.

"Should we go ask her to sit with us?" he asked Eliot.

"No."

"But she's alone."

"Her fault."

Mattie chewed his thumbnail, and as he watched, Caroline turned. Her ponytail swung to the side, exposing a fist-size bald spot at the back of her head. Mattie spit out a bit of thumbnail. "Eliot, I think Delia pulled out some of Caroline's hair."

Eliot stared straight ahead, chewing hard. "Her. Fault."

"But—"

"Hey!" A meaty hand caught Mattie between the shoulder blades and shoved him forward. He barely avoided face-planting in vitamin-enhanced Tater Tots. "Little Larimore!"

"Uh, hey, Doyle." Mattie eased around. "Did you need something?"

"Professor Shelley wants to see you."

"Oh." Mattie couldn't think why she would. He wasn't behind in homework and he wasn't that good with computers.

"Maybe she meant to ask for me," Eliot said to him.

Doyle's eyes narrowed. "Uh, *no*."

Mattie still couldn't think why Professor Shelley would want to see him, and it made him uneasy. He glanced toward Caroline, but Caroline wouldn't look at him, and it made all his insides feel a little heavier.

"Like now, Little Larimore!"

"Oh! Right!" Mattie scrambled off the bench. "I'll see you later, Eliot."

Eliot waved a forkful of something brown before stuffing it into his mouth. "I want to hear everything when you're done."

The hallway outside Professor Shelley's classroom was cool and quiet. Since classes were over for the afternoon, someone had turned off some of the overhead lights and it pooled shadows in all the corners, making the shiny new Munchem look a little like the scary, old Munchem.

The computer lab's door stood open and Mattie ducked inside. The room was empty except for the computers . . . and desks . . . and Delia Dane, who stood in the middle of it all, stroking her silver briefcase like it was a cat. Her blond hair was smooth and tight as ever, but Delia's eyes were too bright and her smile promised mayhem. "Oh, hello, Mattie!" she said loudly.

Mattie stared at her. "Uh, hello to you too. Is Professor Shelley around?" He took another step into the classroom and Delia heaved an enormous gasp.

"What are you doing?" she cried.

Mattie stopped. His teeth began to itch. Something was wrong here. Very wrong. Delia's tone was stuffed full of horror, but she was smiling her nasty smile.

"Is your hair pulled too tight?" Mattie asked. "Where's Professor Shelley? She wanted to see me."

"Mattie?" Professor Shelley's voice drifted over the huge

server cabinet. He could hear her opening and closing doors. "What are you doing here?"

The teeth itching was now joined by a roaring in Mattie's head. What was he *doing* here? Professor Shelley sent for him! "I was told you—"

"Mattie!" Delia cried, sounding as if she had just been confronted with especially hungry zombies. "Don't! Please don't!"

"I'm not doing anything to you!" Mattie yelled, and it was true. Mattie was at least four feet away. He couldn't reach Delia if he stretched his arms as far as they could go.

"Mattie?" Professor Shelley sounded furious. Another cabinet door slammed. "I'll be out in a minute. What are you doing?"

"Nothing!"

Delia's mean little smile turned even meaner. "Stop, Mattie! You'll ruin the computers!"

"WHAT!" Something in the supply room slammed and footsteps slapped the floor. "Mr. Larimore, don't! You! DARE!"

"I'm not doing anything!" To make his point, Mattie took a step back. He was even closer to the door now, nowhere near the computers—and that was when Delia grinned. She pointed one finger to the ceiling fan above her head, and as Mattie watched, it began to turn.

And purple glitter rained down.

It sparkled. It shimmered. It filled the air and coated the computers. It billowed across the carpet. It drifted into the air vent. In short, it went everywhere (as anyone who has ever used glitter knows glitter will do).

Professor Shelley raced out of the server room, black cardigan swirling around her hips. She skidded to a stop, opened her mouth to shriek, and promptly choked on glitter. She coughed and coughed and slammed her fist against her chest. "What happened? What is this?"

Delia's eyes were huge. She pointed toward Mattie, her finger now a sparkling purple. "I tried to stop him! I tried!"

Mattie's blood went cold. Delia's expression was spot-on and her tone was perfect, which in this case meant Delia looked small and vulnerable and her voice had the ideal amount of wobble in it. She was only twelve, but Delia had already perfected the Innocent Look that would serve her well in the coming years.

Professor Shelley gasped. "Mr. Larimore! I expect better from you!"

"I didn't do it!" Mattie protested. "I swear! I was all the way over here!"

"Right next to the power switch!" Delia said and Mattie froze. She was right. By standing in the doorway, he could have easily flipped the lights and fan on, but he hadn't.

She must have some sort of remote, Mattie thought. But how could he get Professor Shelley to check her pockets? Mattie started to speak—and inhaled a bunch of glitter. Now he was coughing too.

Professor Shelley stuck a sparkling purple finger in Mattie's face. "Don't move."

Mattie couldn't if he tried. He thought he was going to cough up a lung, and as Mattie hacked out puffs of purple glitter, Delia stared at her shoes and *laughed*.

"Wow!"

Everyone turned. Eliot stood at the door, blue eyes filled with horror. "What happened? Those poor computers!"

"You!" Professor Shelley launched herself across the room. She ground her words through clenched teeth, and in that moment, she sounded more like a monster than a teacher. "You're behind this, aren't you?"

Eliot pointed at his chest. "Me? Why would I be behind this?"

Professor Shelley coughed tiny gusts of glitter into the air. "Who else would come up with something so horrible?"

Eliot gaped and Mattie knew he didn't have a response to that. Eliot had spent the past several weeks trying to show Professor Shelley what he could do and now—Mattie sneezed— now she thought he was behind this.

"We didn't do it!" Mattie shouted. "Eliot would never mess up a computer!"

"He's been messing up computers all term!" Professor Shelley glared at Eliot. "Admit it, you helped him do this!"

"They couldn't have done it!" Caroline stomped into the classroom, fists clenched. Mattie's knees went wobbly with relief. Caroline might be mad at her brother, but she wasn't going to let him go down for this. "They were with me the whole time," she added.

Mattie peeked at their teacher. The thing was, Caroline was lying, but she was lying so convincingly Professor Shelley had to believe her. After all, it was three denials against Delia's accusation, and when Mattie looked at his teacher's face, he could see she was thinking the same thing.

Then Delia cleared her throat and Professor Shelley flinched. She crossed her arms, staring down at Caroline. "So you're in on it too?"

Eliot stepped in front of his sister. "She would never! And Mattie isn't even supposed to be here! *You* sent for him!"

"I didn't send for him."

"Yes, you did. Doyle . . ." Eliot trailed off, all the color draining from his already pale face. He was putting together what happened. So was Mattie.

First, Delia put the glitter on top of the fan blades. Then she sent Doyle to bring Mattie to the computer lab. Once he was here, she flipped on the fan, and *now* she looked innocent.

Mattie glared at Delia. Delia began to cry. "Why are you looking at me like that?" she wailed.

Pop! Pop! One of the computers shot glitter and smoke through its fan and Professor Shelley screamed.

"Detention!" She cradled the smoldering computer tower in her arms. "All of you!"

Eliot perked up. "With you?"

Mattie had to resist the urge to kick him.

"Oh, no," Professor Shelley said. She crossed both arms and glared down at them, looking a bit like a bedazzled, furious monster. "That would be too easy. Since you three are so interested in making a mess, you can do some cleanup—in the *cemetery.*"

STAY AWAY FROM CREEPY-LOOKING FORESTS

OH, THE MUNCHEM CEMETERY. SURROUNDED BY A SPINY FENCE and filled with tumbledown headstones, it's where teachers bury all the kids who don't graduate. Or maybe not. Maybe it was just something Carter told Mattie to freak him out.

Considering it was Munchem and Carter, either was possible.

Mattie and the Spencers trooped across the overgrown meadow, dragging their rakes. The cemetery lay at the very bottom of the hill, and when Mattie passed through the twisted iron gate, his chest got tight. There was just something about the long yellowy weeds brushing his legs and all the long-dead people under his feet that made Mattie sweat.

But that's the way cemeteries are supposed to be. In fact, if the cemetery had been a person, it would have been very good at its job and it probably would have written all about it on its résumé (which appears to be a document where people write fan fiction about themselves).

But I'm getting distracted and I shouldn't, because Mattie and the Spencers are currently weaving through the old gravestones and feeling distinctly creeped out. When Munchem had been scary and dirty and looked as if it might fall down, the cemetery seemed pretty much appropriate. Now it seemed like a big wart on Munchem's shiny new face.

"You think they'll knock this place down?" Mattie asked the Spencers as they wove through the old gravestones.

"I hope not," Caroline said. "They'll get a nasty surprise if they do."

All three of them looked toward the mausoleum, because behind those chained doors and under the tomb inside the mausoleum was where Headmaster Rooney had kept the real students after he cloned them. After Mattie and the Spencers freed everyone, they didn't know what to do, so they'd locked the place back up. The pods and the computers and the cold, cold concrete were still down there.

"I can't believe Doyle's joined forces with Delia," Mattie said.

"I saw them whispering yesterday." Caroline scratched

behind Beezus's ears, sending fur swirling into the air. "I should have known they were up to something. I can't believe Professor Shelley sided with Delia."

Eliot perked up. "Speaking of Delia, I need some advice. I want to get her a present. Girls like presents, right? What could I get?"

Mattie shrugged. "I have no idea. Caroline?"

"The heads of her enemies," Caroline said, staring straight ahead.

Eliot waved one hand as if to say, *See?* "This is why I don't bother asking her anything," he told Mattie and swiped at the tops of some weeds. Their yellowed heads went flying.

"Eliot . . ." Mattie paused, trying to find the best way to say *How can you* possibly *like Delia?* "How can you *possibly* like Delia? She's awful to Caroline, and she framed me for the glitter bomb."

Eliot nodded sadly. "Yeah."

Mattie narrowed his eyes. "You aren't hearing me. She destroyed those computers!"

Eliot winced. "But if anyone can fix them, Delia can! She's even better than I am with computers—and did you see her throw that elbow at Doyle? She has brains *and* brawn." He paused, thinking. "Maybe we can reform her."

Caroline blew out a winding sigh. "Great, now he wants a project girlfriend."

"Shut it," Eliot told her. "Delia's the total package—so I

need a good gift. You have to help me come up with something, Mattie."

Eliot looked expectantly at Mattie, and Mattie nodded like he would eventually know what to suggest. "We'll figure something out later. After we finish here."

"Great idea."

Mattie was very sure it wasn't, but at least Eliot had shut up about Delia.

"Hurry up," Caroline told them. "I don't want to miss study break"—she narrowed her eyes at Eliot—"with my *friends*."

"Oh, yeah," Eliot said. "The friends you were hanging out with when you followed us to the computer lab."

Mattie swung his rake from his shoulder to the ground. "Shouldn't Professor Shelley come down here to supervise?"

"That would involve leaving her computer lab," Caroline said. "She wants to punish *us*, not her."

Mattie studied the dead leaves coating one of the graves. "Everything is supposed to be new and improved, but is this any different than last term when we used to clean for the teachers?"

"Not really," the Spencers said in unison. They glared at each other.

"Hey," Mattie said, snapping his fingers to get their attention. "What are we going to do about Delia? She really is going to take me down."

The Spencers went silent. Caroline scratched Beezus's back

for a long moment and then said, "Maybe *you* should retaliate. Like, really squish her so good she never messes with you again."

"I'm not really into squishing," Mattie said.

"Yeah," Eliot agreed. "Mattie's more the type who gets squished. Look on the bright side: at least Delia notices you."

Caroline blew out an especially long sigh. "No, the bright side is at least you don't have to live with her."

Now Mattie blew out an especially long sigh. The Spencers, however, didn't notice. They were too busy arguing. Mattie dragged his plastic yard bag to the cemetery's edge and began to rake leaves into it. This far away from Munchem, the trees were closer and darker. Shadows pooled along the forest floor and gathered in the branches. When the wind blew through them, the leaves rubbed together, sounding like a million whispers.

Snap snap!

Mattie jerked and peered into the dim woods. Something was in there. It was heavy and it was *moving*. Mattie swallowed and searched the trees. He spotted squirrel nests, cracked-in-half tree limbs, and a pair of red, red eyes looking straight at him.

"Uh, guys?" Mattie whispered. He his voice caught. *Someone's watching me.*

BEWARE OF YOUR SURROUNDINGS

MATTIE'S VOICE WAS LOCKED INSIDE HIS THROAT. HE TOOK A STEP back and the eyes took a step forward. Branches popped as they were shoved aside. Clone Doyle stepped out of the woods.

Doyle grinned at them. "Hi, Mattie!"

"Hi, Doyle." Mattie slumped. His heart felt like it was trying to pound through his chest. The Spencers dropped their rakes and ran over to see the clone. "You really startled me."

"Sorry about that! Muffin?" Doyle stuck both hands out like he was carrying a tray. Only there was no tray and there were definitely no muffins.

Mattie straightened. "Uh, you feeling okay?"

"I'm great!"

Mattie rather disagreed. Doyle's great big bald head was

dirty. His Munchem uniform hung in tatters, and through those tatters Mattie could see scratches, a smear of bird poop, and more dirt. His eyes were an angry traffic-light red and something black was caked in his teeth. In short, Doyle did not look great. Doyle looked like a hermit who would have a tea party with squirrels.

"Are you sure you're not hungry?" Again, Doyle thrust forward his invisible tray. "The muffins are awfully good!"

"He's lost it," Eliot whispered and his sister shushed him.

Mattie agreed with Eliot, but he wasn't brave enough to say so. Those red eyes had a way of making Mattie's joints feel all shaky. "Are you okay, Doyle? Are you getting upset?"

"No! Of course not!" Doyle cocked his head. "Oh! Is it my eyes?" He blinked twice and the red disappeared, becoming his usual brown. "They do that now. I need a tune-up."

No kidding, Mattie thought. "Wow, uh, have you been out here all this time?"

"Well, sure!" Doyle grinned at them again. "Miss Maple programmed us to stay in the woods. Every day at two o'clock, we have to wait for her here, and you gotta do what you're programmed to do, right?"

"Right," Mattie said weakly. Just the mention of the school secretary made his insides feel cold and slushy. "She's coming back?"

The clone nodded, and Mattie's insides went even colder.

"Has she *been* back?"

"Nope!"

Well, at least that's good, Mattie thought. He studied the clone's blue Munchem trousers. They seemed awfully loose. "You look hungry."

"I *am* hungry. These muffins don't fill me up like they used to—but that's okay because Carter brings us stuff when he can."

Mattie's mouth fell open. "*What?* Why—I mean . . . that's nice of him."

Doyle's face lit up. "It *is* nice of him, and we're nice right back. We bring him stuff too."

Mattie's eyes narrowed as he remembered Carter saying, *Live and let live, you know?* "What kind of stuff?" he asked.

"Candy mostly. There's a gas station a few miles away. Carter says he can't get there and back in time—someone would notice he was gone—so I go for him."

And then Carter sells it to Real Doyle, Real Maxwell, and the rest of the school, Mattie thought, and briefly, he was almost proud—and then he was mostly annoyed because Carter hadn't told Mattie to stay away from the clones to protect him. Carter had told Mattie to stay away so he could continue using them.

"Yeah," Mattie said slowly. "So what do you do when you aren't bringing my brother candy to sell?"

"Oh, you know, baking and counting all the tree branches— I'm up to 2,654,838!"

Mattie didn't know whether to feel sorry for Doyle the Clone or to be amazed with Doyle the Clone. "Wow. That must keep you really busy."

"Completely." Doyle sagged. "It is *exhausting*, but someone's got to do it."

Yeah, this is *so* not good, Mattie thought, and turned to the Spencers. The Spencers looked as if they quite agreed with Mattie.

"Hey, Doyle, do you think you could tell me how many branches are over there?" Mattie pointed to a thicket of small trees.

Doyle brightened. "Of course I could tell you!" He trotted toward the trees and began counting aloud. "One . . . two . . . three . . ."

Mattie and the Spencers watched. "Remember when you said we shouldn't do anything?"

Caroline winced. "Fine, you're right. We can't leave him here."

Mattie nodded. "I know."

"But we can't take him back with us."

"I *know*."

Doyle pointed to the branches above his head. "Sixteen . . . seventeen . . . eighteen . . ."

"Maybe it's not so bad out here," Mattie said slowly. "I mean, he gets lots of fresh air."

Eliot shuddered. "Oh yeah? If the outdoors are so great, why are bugs always trying to come inside?"

Caroline studied her brother. "You really were scarred by Boy Scout camp, weren't you?"

"I have been telling you this for years!" Eliot gasped, face lightning up with an idea. "I know what we can do! We can take him apart!"

"No *way*," Mattie said. "He's practically a person. We don't know where the robot stuff ends and the human stuff begins."

Eliot frowned. "True—although you could say that's an excellent reason to find out."

"No!" Caroline and Mattie shouted in unison.

Eliot wilted. "'Noooooo, Eliot,'" he muttered to himself. "'You can't have a clone. No, Eliot, you can't take a clone apart. No, no, no.' That's all you ever hear." He stomped off to help Doyle. Mattie watched nervously until he was sure Eliot wasn't reaching for Doyle's control panel.

"Maybe we could find someone to take him," Mattie said at last. "Like, a nice family with a farm where he could wander."

"Is this like when my dad said he was sending my dog to a farm?" Caroline crossed her arms. "Because that wasn't a farm; he had him put to sleep."

"No, I really was thinking about a farm." Mattie paused, a worrisome thought occurring to him. He lifted his voice: "Hey, Doyle? Are there any more clones in the woods with you?"

Doyle nodded. "Maxwell is here too. Everyone else went with Miss Maple. Forty-one . . . forty-two . . . forty-three . . ."

"Ugh," Mattie muttered. "That makes it even more complicated. I don't know what to do."

Caroline frowned. Clearly, she didn't either, and that made Mattie feel even worse. They couldn't leave the clones. They couldn't take the clones with them. They had to do *something*. But what?

"Okay," Mattie said finally. "Um, Doyle?"

"Yes?"

"You don't have to do what Miss Maple says anymore, okay? She's gone." Mattie watched the clone's face twitch as he absorbed the words.

"Are you sure?" Doyle asked at last. "Because that sounds like you might be malfunctioning too. We're programmed to listen only to Miss Maple."

Mattie paused. "How exactly did she program you?"

Doyle's eyes flashed. "Like this!" He fumbled with the back of his neck, turning so Mattie and the Spencers could see a small flesh-colored panel hidden beneath his collar. It popped open, revealing computer bits that made zero sense to Mattie, but made Eliot gasp and clap his hands together.

Mattie eyed his friend. "Think you could reprogram him?"

"Is the Pope Catholic?"

"Yes?"

Eliot gave him a disgusted look and hurried over to Doyle.

For several minutes, there was nothing but the sounds of Eliot muttering and something beeping. "Okay," Eliot said at last, shutting the panel and backing away. "What are you going to do when you see people other than us?"

"Hide," Doyle said.

"And what will you make Maxwell do?" Eliot asked.

"I'll make Maxwell hide too—wait, does this mean we can't talk to Carter anymore? He's very nice. I would miss him."

"No," Mattie said. "You can still talk to Carter, but no one else, okay? You have to stay a secret. We're going to help you."

Caroline tugged at her ponytail. "How are we going to feed them, *and* not get caught, *and* what if"—she dropped her voice to a hiss—"what if Miss Maple comes back?"

Mattie thought for a moment. "I don't know, but I do know I've got this. Somehow."

But even Mattie knew he was in way over his head.

IF YOU GET CAUGHT, THERE ARE CONSEQUENCES, SO YOU SHOULD, YOU KNOW, AVOID THAT

THE LONG WALK BACK UP THE OVERGROWN MEADOW TOWARD the school wasn't long enough. Mattie needed a plan to deal with Delia, a plan to deal with the clones, and a plan to deal with the glitter that seemed to be stuck in his ears. Honestly? It was too much planning. Mattie's head felt overstuffed.

Or maybe that was just the pollen. It was *everywhere.*

Mattie followed the Spencers through the courtyard gate as a gust of mucus yellow pollen billowed over them. Everyone sneezed.

"Do you remember it being this bad last year?" Eliot asked his sister.

Caroline ignored him, and it reminded Mattie he had yet

another plan to come up with: making the Spencers like each other again.

"Mattie!"

Mattie looked up. His father was charging their way, dragging Carter behind him. Fresh sweat broke out between Mattie's shoulder blades, because somewhere between purple glitter and dirty clones, he had entirely forgotten about getting in trouble with Professor Shelley.

But Mattie remembered everything now and everything made him panic.

He swallowed. "This is so not good."

"I want to talk to you!" Mr. Larimore was also sweating. It tended to happen a lot when he was mad or running or, in this case, mad *and* running. He clutched Carter by his upper arm and used his free hand to shake a finger at his youngest son. "What were you thinking?"

Mattie didn't even know where to begin. The Spencers didn't seem to either. They looked at each other and then they looked at Mattie. They wanted to run and Mattie didn't blame them. He wanted to run too.

"Maybe you should go," he whispered.

"Are you sure?" Caroline's eyes were enormous.

"He's sure!" her brother said and grabbed her arm. Eliot dragged Caroline away as Mr. Larimore stomped closer, a sullen Carter stomping along after him.

Mr. Larimore jammed a finger in Mattie's face. "Do you have any idea how much money it will take to clean and fix those computers? And don't even get me started on Professor Shelley! I thought the blasted woman was going to burn down my office. You know how she is about her computer lab."

Mattie did indeed. In fact, the memory of Professor Shelley bellowing at him was quite fresh in his mind. "Dad, I didn't do it! I swear!"

"Of course you did it! Professor Shelley saw you!"

"She didn't see anything!" Mattie burst out. "She's just agreeing with Delia and Delia's lying!"

Mr. Larimore went very still. "That's a serious accusation, Mattie. Why would either of them lie? What do they have to gain from it?"

Mattie opened his mouth, then shut it. He had no idea. "I didn't do it," he said at last.

"Well, Professor Shelley said you did."

"What's going on?" Carter asked, brushing the wrinkles out of his sleeve. "What'd he do anyway?"

"Mattie poured glitter on the ceiling fan blades." Mr. Larimore took a heaving, wheezing breath. "When they were turned on, the glitter went everywhere."

Carter's mouth hung so far open, Mattie could see his back teeth. "Wow," he said. "Go big or go home, huh? *Nice.*"

Mattie caught himself grinning. Wait. Nice? It wasn't nice. It was horrible—and Mattie hadn't actually done it—but somehow when Carter grinned at him like that, Mattie felt a million feet tall.

"Nice?" Mr. Larimore's eyes bugged and his forehead vein bulged. "It isn't nice! It's destructive! It's indecent! It's *bad*!"

Their father took a moment's breath and fished a handkerchief from his pocket. He mopped his shiny bald head. Carter glanced at Mattie and winked.

Just like before, Mattie was suddenly soaring, and just like before, it bothered him. It seemed like he couldn't win. To make his dad proud, he had to be a good kid, and that made his brother mad. To make his brother proud, he had to be a bad kid, and that upset his dad.

I don't know how to fit, Mattie thought, but he didn't get to think it for long because Mr. Larimore was drawing himself up for another lecture.

"Boys! You can't act like this!" Their father wiped his head again. "It makes me look unfit. It makes Munchem look unfit. You two are supposed to be reformed. Carter"—Mr. Larimore turned to his oldest son—"you had finally turned a corner. You were doing so much better."

Mattie looked at his feet. Mr. Larimore had confused the Real Carter with the Clone Carter. It was an understandable mistake—even more understandable when Mattie and Carter remembered Mr. Larimore had no idea Headmaster Rooney had been making clones—but it was still an uncomfortable mistake because no matter how much Carter enjoyed angering his parents, deep down Mattie was pretty sure Carter also wanted them to notice when he wasn't, well, Carter.

"I need to go back home for a few days," Mr. Larimore continued, and as he did, a pale face appeared at the window above them. It was so pale it could have been a ghost, but unfortunately for Mattie, it wasn't a ghost at all. It was worse. It was Delia. Her slicked-down blond hair flashed in the afternoon sunlight and then she disappeared. "I need to see your mother," Mr. Larimore said. "I need to order more computers. And I have to check in with the office. So you two better behave."

Mattie nodded. "I'll be good. There won't be a problem," he said, and there wouldn't be as long as Mattie figured out how to deal with the clones, the Spencers, and his little Delia Dane issue.

Maybe not so little, Mattie thought, searching the windows again. Thankfully, Delia was gone.

Mr. Larimore turned back for the school. A narrow chauffeur waited for him at the top of the hill and Mr. Larimore stomped toward him, wiping his head and muttering under his breath.

Carter watched their dad go, and slapped Mattie on the shoulder. "Good job with the glitter," he said quietly. "I didn't think you had it in you."

Mattie wilted. Technically, he didn't. Delia did. Mattie scowled at his brother. "I know about the clones and the candy, Carter," he whispered.

Carter frowned. "Yeah, about that . . ."

"That's all you have to say? Doyle looks hungry. When's the last time you fed him?"

Carter had to think about it.

"You can't just forget to feed him!" Mattie whispered furiously.

"I didn't forget the clones. When I need something from them, I'll bring them something. That's how business works."

Mattie slumped. *Fine.* He would feed the clones. Somehow. He glanced at his brother. "You really don't care if Munchem closes? Last term, you helped us save it. You said you didn't want to go to military school."

"That was before I found out Dad was going to be here all the time. I think I'd rather take my chances with a drill sergeant."

Mattie looked at him and Carter sighed. "Okay, yes, I don't want to go to military school, but I can't take him always being here. He drives me crazy." Carter shook his head, shaggy dark hair flying. "Anyway, things are going to get better."

"Why's that?"

"Because now Dad's gone. It's time to have some fun." Carter rubbed his hands together. "I've been good for far too long, Mattie. It's been hard. I've nearly strained something."

"Uh, maybe you should try a little harder."

Carter laughed. "This is going to be great."

KEEP YOUR FRIENDS CLOSE
AND YOUR UNDERWEAR CLOSER

MATTIE WOULD NEVER HAVE THOUGHT DISCOVERING CLONE DOYLE would be a good thing, but it was. Caroline and Eliot stayed so busy brainstorming ideas to sneak the clones food, they forgot they hated each other.

Maybe things are finally getting back to normal, Mattie thought as he waited for history class to end. Up by the whiteboard, Lem was helping Dr. Hoo test new foods, and as Mattie watched, one of the newly developed sausages tried to wiggle off the plate. Dr. Hoo stabbed it with a fork.

Well, Mattie thought, it's as back to normal as it gets around Munchem.

The scientists sat at a slate-topped table in front of the classroom, plastic plates piled with food spread out in front of them. Dr. Hoo took a forkful of something purple and put it in his mouth.

"How's that one taste?" Lem asked, pencil poised above his paper.

Dr. Hoo chewed for a moment. "Like regret in the morning."

Lem nodded, scribbling something in his notebook. "And the other?"

Another forkful. This time, the stuff was green. There was more chewing and more thinking. "Tastes like feet," Dr. Hoo said at last, swallowing. "Sweaty feet."

Mattie felt his eyes bug, but Lem wrote down Dr. Hoo's observation without even blinking.

"I still think it's simpler just to steal a few extra sandwiches or burgers from the cafeteria," Caroline whispered as she pretended to get something out of her book bag. "We can stick them under our shirts. Trust me. No one notices—and if they do, they just think you're chubby."

Mattie and Eliot nodded. After all, Caroline would know.

"I agree," Mattie whispered. "If we all take something at each meal, we'll have enough, but how do we get down there regularly?"

"We could drug the teachers," Eliot whispered. "Make them go to sleep. They'll never know we were gone."

Mattie studied his friend for a moment. Eliot was a great kid. He was smart and he was loyal, but every once in a while he was also scary. "Yeah, so moving on."

"If you keep watch," Caroline whispered, "I could sneak down there and back. You could do some sort of signal so I would know when it was safe to come up."

"Who's whispering?" Lem asked, lifting his head to see across the rows of students. "Does someone have a question?"

Mattie and the Spencers went back to their work. Or what passed as work at Munchem these days. It was the last part of American History and everyone was finishing up their Dream Bear questionnaires.

The Dream Bear in question sat on the edge of Lem's desk, its fangs hanging down and its claws lying out. The teddy was supposed to scare away children's nightmares, but Mattie was pretty sure it was going to *give* him nightmares. He concentrated on his questionnaire.

> *Would you or your family be likely to purchase Dream Bear in the future?*

No way, Mattie wrote.

> *Would you or your family be likely to purchase Dream Bear as a gift?*

Only if I didn't like the person, Mattie wrote.

> *How would you improve Dream Bear?*

Mattie looked from the toy's claws to its fangs to its beady little eyes. There was so much to cover and yet the questionnaire's answer blank was so small. He sighed, working in silence until the bell rang.

"Questionnaires!" Lem cried as the students surged to their feet. Doyle and Maxwell tried to duck past him. "Don't forget to turn in your questionnaires!"

Mattie and the Spencers grabbed their bags as everyone stuffed their questionnaires into Lem's outstretched hands. The scientist scrambled to keep the papers from falling on the floor.

"We will caucus again on Monday," Lem shouted. "For those of you who don't know what caucus means—"

It was too late. Everyone had spilled into the hallway. Mattie and the Spencers followed the crowd of students out the doors and onto Munchem's lawn. It had been a long week, and when Mattie tilted his face toward the sun, he could almost forget about Delia and clones and how his dad might close Munchem.

Mattie squinted at the sky. Fat-bottomed clouds drifted over the school. They were especially puffy today—especially puffy and *foot shaped*?

Mattie stared, and as he stared the foot cloud began to blur in the wind. It still looked like a foot, but now it looked like a foot that was partially dissolved in acid.

Well, that's disturbingly realistic, Mattie thought, tilting his head and watching the cloud's edges turn pink. Like blood, Mattie thought with a shudder. He was so busy thinking it, he wasn't watching where he was going. But, honestly, even if he had been watching, he wouldn't have expected to see a balloon hit him in the face.

Or for that balloon to be carrying one of his dirty socks.

"What the—?" Mattie snatched at the balloon and the striped sock came loose in his hand. Mattie gaped at it—and then gaped at the schoolyard. There must have been fifty balloons bumping along the ground and drifting listlessly against Munchem's brick walls.

Each one had a different piece of clothing taped to it. Mattie's shirts were attached to blue balloons, his socks were attached to yellow balloons, and his pants were attached to big green balloons.

A spring breeze stirred through the grass and Caroline caught a yellow balloon as it passed. "Uh, you want this?" she asked as other students began to wander into the schoolyard. Mattie snatched his sock and stuffed it in his pocket. He grabbed a passing shirt and crammed it under his arm.

"Uh, Mattie?" It was Caroline again and she did not sound happy. "I think you might want to grab that."

Mattie turned, and wheezed as his *underwear* floated past on pink balloons!

"Oh, that's not good," Eliot said, wide-eyed.

Not good? It was awful. Mattie's underwear shimmied in the breeze, drifting toward a huddle of eighth grade girls. They shrieked and ran. Mattie ran too. He ran left to grab his pants. He ran right to grab his underwear. He was so busy running to catch his clothes, he didn't have a chance to thank the Spencers, who were helping.

That's one of the great things about friends. Sometimes they aren't just the people you sit with during lunch. Sometimes they're the people who grab your dirty socks before they hit someone in the face.

The breeze suddenly picked up and Mattie had to dive to grab his gym shorts. He hit the grass with both knees and caught the balloon, and he almost had his shorts free when he heard the laughter.

Not just any laughter. *This* laughter was mean and a little maniacal. In fact, it was the kind of laughter you might use if you were an evil scientist and just had an evil scientist breakthrough. In this case though there weren't any scientists (evil or otherwise) standing in the schoolyard. It was only Delia, and she was laughing so hard she was wiping tears from her eyes.

Mattie's intuition went itchy and his face went bright red. Delia was behind this. He just knew it.

The girl's laughter turned to giggles and the giggles turned to hiccups and she walked off. Mattie watched her go—or at least he watched until another pair of pants hit him in the shoulder.

"Mattie?" Caroline asked.

"Yeah?"

"I might have been wrong when I said you wouldn't have a problem with Delia."

KNOW YOUR ENEMY

I MIGHT HAVE BEEN WRONG WHEN I SAID YOU WOULDN'T HAVE a problem with Delia.

It was the understatement of the century and Mattie didn't know what to say. Then again, what could he say? It isn't every day you have problems with balloons and your underwear and your underwear being taped to those balloons.

It isn't every day when Caroline Spencer admits she was wrong too.

Yes, indeed, this was uncharted territory for Mattie, and he didn't know what to do. "Why is she doing this?" he managed at last.

"Maybe she likes you," Eliot said, and he sounded so mournful Mattie wanted to thump him. Thankfully, he couldn't.

His arms were too full of clothes. "Maybe it's Delia's way of flirting. We don't know. I can't get her to pay attention to me at all."

Mattie and Caroline exchanged a look.

"I would gladly trade places with you if I could," Mattie said at last, reminding himself that Eliot was his best friend and being best friends meant you had to overlook a few things— even if one of those things was your best friend being in love with your worst enemy. "But somehow I don't think stringing up my underwear means Delia likes me."

"Good point."

Mattie looked at Caroline. "This is bad," he said. And because this was Munchem, where things always go from bad to worse, another cloud of mucus yellow pollen billowed past them. Mattie coughed. Eliot was right about nature being awful.

"What am I going to do?" Mattie asked Caroline.

"Lock up your underwear for starters."

"I mean about *Delia*."

"What the . . . ?" Everyone turned around. Carter stood on the walk, one arm around a girl's shoulders. Carter's eyes bugged and the girl giggled.

"It's not what it looks like," Mattie said—although he had no idea why he said it. It was exactly what it looked like: his clothes were strapped to balloons and the balloons were drifting around the schoolyard.

Carter looked at another pair of floating underwear, then he looked at Mattie, then he looked at the floating underwear again.

"Mattie," his brother said at last, shaking his head. "We gotta talk."

We gotta talk. Those of you with boyfriends and girlfriends and evil sidekicks will know the horrible dip your stomach makes when someone says those words, and for those of you who don't? You will.

We gotta talk is a variation on the universally unpleasant *We need to talk*, and both of those are code for *You're in trouble. I'm going to talk and you're going to listen.*

In instances like these, it's important to pick the right location for your talk: crowded restaurants, crowded water parks, and even crowded grocery stores are ideal. Why? Because they're crowded. You have witnesses.

And since Carter didn't have any of those places, he took Mattie and the Spencers into the dead gardens and made his little brother sit on one of the mossy benches.

"Mattie, we gotta talk about what's been going on." Carter folded both hands behind his back and began to pace back and forth on the grass. The Spencers watched him with interest.

Mattie watched him with dread. "This latest issue with Delia? It isn't good. It isn't good at all."

Mattie agreed, but Carter's tone seemed to suggest *he* was the one whose underwear had just been seen by half the school.

His brother stopped pacing. He stood in front of Mattie and shook one finger at him. "Look, now that we're friends, I have to stick up for you, but I'm not going to beat up Delia."

Mattie paled. "I wouldn't want you to."

"I have a code, Mattie, and that code includes not hitting girls."

Another gust of yellow pollen drifted over them and Mattie sneezed. He wondered what else Carter's code involved, but Mattie didn't get to ask because his brother kept going.

"And because of my code," Carter continued, "I'm going to teach you how to do better, how to *be* better."

And how to sound like their dad? Because, at that moment, Carter sounded—and looked—almost exactly like Mr. Larimore. Mattie, however, was smart enough not to say it.

"What are you talking about?" Caroline asked. "We need to figure out how to pay Delia back."

"*And* why she's out to get me," Mattie added.

"What do you think I'm coming to?" Carter paused, collecting himself. "Mattie, here at Munchem, everyone's a criminal. We fight. We lie."

"That's true," Eliot said. "I lie all the time."

Caroline shrugged. "I only lie when I have to."

"Enough!" Carter waved one hand and everyone went quiet. "Now, I was going to start with the basics, but clearly we don't have time to find lighter fluid and a waffle iron, so I'm going straight to the big stuff."

Mattie shifted nervously. "Big stuff?"

"Yep, big stuff." His brother paused again and Mattie decided Carter got his flair for dramatics from their mother. "Mattie," Carter said at last, pulling a tiny vial from his pocket. "You need *this*."

Everyone fell silent. Carter made the vial sound amazing, like Mattie needed to pull a sword from a stone, but the thing was, there was nothing amazing about a tiny plastic bottle filled with clear liquid.

"I don't get it," Eliot announced.

Carter dangled the vial in Mattie's face. "Put a few drops of this in Delia's food and it will give her the most epic diarrhea she's ever had."

"What is it?" Mattie asked.

Carter grinned. "Do you really want to know?"

"Well, I know it's gross," Caroline said.

Mattie agreed, but he was also ever so slightly kinda sorta interested too. Having your underwear put on display for half the school can do that to you. Mattie thought about it. He stared at the bottle. He stared at his brother. He held out his hand.

Carter snatched the vial back. "You want it? You pay for it. Ten bucks."

Mattie gaped. "For that tiny thing?"

"Ten dollars compensates me for my risk." Carter rolled the bottle from hand to hand. "I'm not supposed to be selling stuff, but I can't ignore my fellow students' need." He paused. "I'm a giver, you see."

"I don't have any money and you know it."

Carter sighed, and held out the bottle. "Fine, you can consider it a loan."

Mattie hesitated. This was his chance. This was . . . "I can't. I don't want to make her sick. There has to be another way."

"You have very limited thinking, do you know that?" Carter said. "After the glitter bomb, I thought you were really going somewhere."

"That wasn't me," Mattie said miserably. "That was Delia too."

"Oh. Well. That does change things."

Mattie wilted a bit. He really couldn't win these days.

Carter put one hand on Mattie's shoulder. "If you don't want my brilliant suggestions, fine. But think this through. You need to beat Delia at her own game, and she's clearly better than you are. She's a bad kid, probably a future criminal, and how do you beat criminals?"

Mattie thought for a moment. "You become a better criminal."

BEWARE OF AMBUSHES AND ALSO
BUSHES THAT CAN BE USED FOR AMBUSHES

TRUER WORDS WERE NEVER SPOKEN. WELL, PERHAPS, TRUER WORDS were spoken when Mattie's mother said it is better to be kind than right, but it could go either way really.

Regardless, we've reached another important moment in Mattie's life. Only he had no idea it was important at all. Isn't it interesting how Mattie's evolution into the world's greatest criminal didn't happen all at once? It wasn't just one big decision that led him to his destiny. It was a thousand tiny decisions that got him there. And, luckily for you, I know all of them—unlike other biographers I could name. Fine, I'll name him: Alistair Wicket.

It isn't like he can read anyway.

Ahem. Now back to Mattie, who was currently sitting through Dr. Hoo's language arts class. I say "sitting" rather than "learning" or "listening" or even "setting things on fire" because Dr. Hoo hated teaching Language Arts. In fact, he had taken just that moment to remind the students.

"Like you're ever going to use this!" He shook a handful of their book reports. "Because let me tell you: magical springs that make you immortal? Way harder than you would think. Ask me how I know—no, really, ask me."

Dr. Hoo paused, gasping for breath. He looked expectantly at the students and the students slouched deeper in their chairs. No one wanted to ask.

Mattie slid even lower. The Language Arts hallway and classrooms smelled terrible. It was like a mix between body odor and mildew, but worse. Mattie pulled the neck of his T-shirt over his nose and mouth. It didn't help. He could still smell it.

Next to him, Eliot took several deep breaths. "I don't know what that scent is, but I do know it isn't moldy laundry."

"It's worse." Caroline gagged.

Dr. Hoo walked between the desks, passing out papers. He paused next to Mattie. "Why do you look like you're going to be sick? What's wrong?"

Where would Mattie even begin? With the clones in the woods? With his Delia Dane problem? With the fact that he was pretty sure his nostrils were blistering from stench?

Dr. Hoo narrowed his eyes. "Are you stressed about the upcoming exam?"

Yeah, let's go with that, Mattie thought. He nodded.

"Don't be." Dr. Hoo put a chilled hand on Mattie's shoulder and squeezed. Mattie was pretty sure Dr. Hoo was going for Reassuring Professor, but really it just felt like Being Patted by a Zombie. "I never studied," Dr. Hoo continued. "I failed exams. I never did my homework. And did I pursue my dream anyway?"

"Yes?" Mattie guessed.

"No."

"Oh." Mattie hesitated. "Uh, are you happy about that?"

"Also no."

Mattie nodded like this made complete and total sense, and to his complete and total relief, Dr. Hoo patted his shoulder once more and moved on. Mattie glanced at the Spencers.

"Is it just me or is he getting weirder?" Caroline whispered.

Eliot nodded. "Kent said he wigged out last week, went on some rant about how no one appreciates his genius."

The electronic bell began to chime and everyone scrambled from their desks, eager to get away, and who could blame them? It was Friday, it was sunny, and that side of the school smelled like death warmed over.

Outside, Mattie turned his face toward the sun, and for several seconds, forgot all about everything that was happening.

Which made Delia's timing that much worse.

"Hello, losers," she said.

Mattie and the Spencers turned around as Delia swept out of the bushes—or, rather, *tried* to sweep out of the bushes. It was a good hiding spot, but not so great for stylish entrances, and she had to tug twigs from her sweater. Delia paused, one hand on her hip. Her collared shirt was partially untucked, her smirk was awful, and next to her were Doyle and Maxwell, who stood on either side of her like grumpy bookends.

"Did you enjoy all the glitter, Little Larimore?" Delia asked, strolling closer. "The balloons?"

Mattie scowled. "What do you think?"

"That I have brilliant ideas," she said.

Caroline launched forward and Mattie grabbed her arm. It made Delia laugh like she was some sort of fairy-tale princess.

How does she do that? Mattie wondered. Most days, there was something very shiny about the girl. Maybe it was her hair: very blond. Maybe it was her smile: awfully white. Maybe it was the buttons on her school jacket: very, *very* gold.

Whatever it was, it wasn't her personality. Because even though Delia might look like a fairy-tale princess and she might sound like a fairy-tale princess, Mattie had never known anyone so fairy-tale-villain-ish.

He stepped in front of Caroline. "Why are you picking on us?" The question had sounded better in Mattie's head. When it came out of his mouth, it was small and whiny. It made him even angrier. "It isn't my fault you're here. I haven't done anything to you."

That sounded even worse. Mattie frowned. He was having a terrible day for sounding tough.

"Of course you have." Delia patted her glossy hair. It was slicked down like a helmet. "*You're* the reason I'm stuck here, and *you*"—she glared at Caroline, who glared right back—"*you* didn't want to be my friend. I can't have that."

"No, she can't," Maxwell said. Delia narrowed her eyes at him and Maxwell looked at the ground.

"See? Even Maxwell knows how these things work," Delia continued. "I'm the New Kid, and that means everyone is watching. I had to make an example of you so people would know I'm not to be messed with."

Mattie rolled his eyes. "Fine, you made your point. No one will mess with you. Now leave us alone."

"I will if you do something for me," she said.

"Like what?" he asked.

Delia smiled.

The tiny voice inside Mattie's head—the one that occasionally encouraged him to steal subway trains, but mostly had much better ideas—whispered, *You are so not going to like what she's about to say.*

Delia walked slowly up to Mattie. "It's *your* fault the cloning plan didn't work," she whispered in his ear. Behind her,

Maxwell and Doyle glanced nervously at each other. "And I want the clones, Mattie."

Mattie's heart thudded hard. "What?"

"I want the clones," Delia repeated softly. "I *know* you know where they are, and I want them."

Mattie pulled back. "I have no idea what you're talking about," he announced, almost grinning because the lie was *good*. It sounded very convincing, the absolute perfect combination of confused and adamant.

Carter would be so proud, he thought.

"You're lying," Delia said through clenched teeth. "You know exactly what I'm talking about. My sources told me all about what you did."

"Your sources?" Mattie pretended to think. He even scratched his head to really look confused. "Caroline? Do you know what she's talking about?"

"Nope." Caroline shook her head.

Mattie turned to Eliot. "Eliot?"

Eliot heaved an enormous sigh. "No," he said at last.

Mattie looked back at Delia. "We have no idea what you're talking about. Maybe you should ask Headmaster Rooney—or my dad. I'm sure they would *love* to talk to you about it."

Delia ground her teeth, making the muscles in her jaw twitch. "You're going to do exactly what I say or *else*, Mattie Larimore."

Mattie felt a surge in his chest. It might have been bravery. It might have been stupidity. Either way, he leaned forward. "Or else you'll do *what*?"

Delia leaned forward too. Their noses touched. "I'll destroy you, bit by bit."

Now it was Mattie's turn to smirk. "Bring it."

BE CAREFUL WHAT YOU WISH FOR

THEY WERE BOLD WORDS AND MATTIE FELT GOOD ABOUT SAYING them. That didn't last, of course. Some of this is because it's Munchem and nothing good ever lasts at Munchem, but the rest of it is Delia Dane. Now, mind you, if I had been Delia's biographer, I would have taken the opportunity to explain that when she shredded all the Dream Bear prototypes, Delia was really doing the world a favor.

But because she picked Alistair Wicket as her biographer, I will stick to the absolute truth: the bears were there, and Delia needed something fast to bring Mattie around. It might not have been as sparkly as the glitter incident, but it definitely had a message: do what I want, or you're next.

"It's almost poetic," Caroline whispered to Mattie as they watched shredded Dream Bear bits float through the air. "The girl's horrible, but she's good with a scene."

Eliot nodded. "Definite flair for the dramatic."

"Quick too," Caroline added. "Hasn't even been twenty-four hours."

"Yep," Eliot said. "She's fast."

Once again, the Spencers were agreeing with each other, but Mattie didn't get to enjoy it. In fact, he didn't think he was going to get to enjoy anything ever again, because Professor Shelley was striding toward them. Her heavy black boots clunked like hooves on the shiny floorboards. There was no escape.

Mattie sighed and turned to his friends. "I really should have seen this coming."

The Spencers said nothing. Of course, there really wasn't anything to say. When you tell someone to bring it, you have to be prepared for the worst. It was a major misstep, but entirely understandable, because while Mattie would one day grow up to be a diabolical master thief, at this point in his life he was still a good kid and good kids never see the bad kids coming.

Or something like that. Bottom line, Mattie and the Spencers were watching Dream Bear fluff roll past like tumbleweed, Professor Shelley was almost to them, and up in her dorm room, Delia Dane was laughing and laughing.

It's true. She was. Check the sixty-third chapter of her

second biography. It discusses the situation at length—in fact, it's probably too much length because Alistair Wicket wrote it and everyone knows he can't shut up.

But at the moment, Professor Shelley was stomping up to Mattie. She glared down at him. "What on earth did you do?"

"How do you know we aren't innocent bystanders?" Caroline demanded. "What happened to 'innocent until proven guilty'?"

Once again, Mattie saw a flicker of agreement in their computer science teacher's face.

She's not positive we did it, he realized.

"Mattie Larimore," Professor Shelley said, her face paler and waxier than usual. "Admit what you did and I'll only give you another cemetery detention. If you don't . . ." The professor trailed off menacingly, her already dark eyes going darker.

But I *didn't* do it, Mattie thought, opening his mouth to say so. It was automatic. It was understandable.

It was also when Mattie got an idea. He could lie and say he shredded the Dream Bears. He could tell the truth and deny he shredded the Dream Bears.

Or he could remember that Professor Shelley's worst punishment was cleaning up the cemetery, and the clones needed to be fed, and if he admitted to shredding the Dream Bears, he could make Delia's revenge work for him instead of against him.

It was a rather complicated idea when Mattie thought

about it like that, but some days, that's just how ideas go.

He took a deep breath, looked at Professor Shelley, and shrugged. "Yeah, I did it."

"And I helped," Caroline said, stepping forward.

"Me too," Eliot added.

Their teacher stood a little taller, which was very tall indeed, and pointed a finger at Mattie and the Spencers. "Detention! Now!"

"I can't believe you backed me up," Mattie said to Caroline as they pulled plastic leaf bags from the garden shed's shelves. The bags kept sticking on the shelf ledge and Mattie had to yank—and then yank again. "You knew I didn't shred those stupid bears."

Caroline nodded, eyes on the canisters of rat poison Rupert had left on the floor. "Yeah."

"Totally," her brother said.

Mattie stared at them. "Did *you* shred them?"

Caroline rolled her eyes as high as they would go. "Of course not!"

"Then why— Did you know what I was thinking? About how I was going to feed the clones?"

"No." She scooped up all the rat poison canisters and dumped them into the garbage, hiding them under a fertilizer bag. "But I also knew you had to be up to something, otherwise you never would've violated your Good Kid title."

"I don't have a title."

"You so do," Eliot said.

"Not anymore," Caroline said, stepping around Eliot. "It was pretty clever getting thrown into detention so we could feed the clones. Wish I'd thought of it."

"Me too."

The Spencers studied each other, sharing a look Mattie didn't know how to interpret until Eliot suddenly said: "Sorry."

"Me too," Caroline said.

"I still like her," Eliot added.

"I still hate her."

"Fair enough." Eliot turned to Mattie. "Now what?"

Mattie shook his head. It was kind of amazing. Maybe even more than *kind of,* because for all the Spencers' bickering, they always had Mattie's back—even when they didn't know what he was doing. Carter might be disappointed in Mattie, Mr. Larimore might be furious, and Munchem might close, but some things stayed bigger and truer than any of that. In later years, Mattie would tell the *Quality Thief's Quarterly* he'd been lonely before the Spencers—and he hadn't known it—but being with the Spencers just fit.

And, coincidentally, being with the Spencers also made it much, much easier to steal the queen's jewels.

It was just like all those movies and books said: things were just better with friends. Even so, Mattie felt guilty about dragging them into his issues with Delia.

"This is my fault," Mattie said, holding open the garden shed door so the Spencers could pass. Outside, the sun beat down on them, catching Mattie's dark hair. It made him feel like his skull was cooking. Clever move or not, it was going to be a long, hot day of cleanup. "I shouldn't have antagonized her—and I should've seen it coming."

"Whatever," Eliot said, striding through the courtyard gate. "Destroying those Dream Bears actually did the world a favor."

"*I* didn't destroy them."

"You're going to get credit though. It's almost as good." Eliot tapped a finger against his chin, thinking. "Maybe it's *better.*"

Mattie slung his rake over his shoulder and kicked at a patch of weeds. With every step, the foil-wrapped vitamin burgers rubbed his tummy, making it itch. "My dad is going to kill me when he gets back. I've never gotten in so much trouble."

"I don't know," Caroline said, tugging at her ponytail. "The subway thing was a pretty big deal."

"I meant quantity, not quality," Mattie explained.

"Oh."

"I'm supposed to be helping save Munchem," he continued. "Not destroy it."

"You're *not* destroying it," Caroline told him. "And technically, you *are* saving it because you're keeping everyone from finding out there are clones living in the woods, and a cloning machine down in the basement, and a headmaster who still can't remember any of it thanks to us."

Caroline turned her face toward the sky—a sky empty of clouds, foot-shaped or otherwise—and took a deep breath, basking in the sunshine. She looked so relaxed she could have been talking about tea parties or Beezus's medicated baths. "Besides," Caroline added, "I think you did a great job standing up to Delia and I'm glad you did it. Someone needed to."

Mattie wasn't so sure this was a great job of standing up to someone, but he appreciated the sentiment all the same.

"How does Delia do it?" Caroline asked. "She was sitting in our dorm when I left. She couldn't have gotten down there in time."

"Doyle and Maxwell?" Mattie suggested. "Or maybe it was one of her 'sources.'"

"I still don't know what she's talking about."

"Me neither." Mattie paused, thinking. "It's someone who knows about last term, so that could be any of the teachers . . . Rooney . . . Miss Maple . . . maybe even one of the clones who escaped with her."

"You don't *know* it's Delia behind the Dream Bears," Eliot said.

Mattie and Caroline glared at him.

"Why would she want the clones anyway?" Caroline continued.

"I don't know," Mattie said. "Maybe she wants to make an army of Delias. Isn't that what bad guys do in movies? I could totally see Delia being a bad guy."

Caroline shuddered. "You can't let her have Maxwell and Doyle. It would be worse than giving them to Eliot."

"Hey!" Behind them, Eliot swatted at the tops of weeds.

"I thought you were ignoring me," Caroline said. "Besides, it's true."

Her brother sighed and said nothing, probably because even though he was in love with Delia, he could also see Caroline's point. Eliot had a lot of good intentions, but none of them applied to the clones.

"I'm going to get Delia back for this," Mattie said as they passed through the crooked cemetery gate. "I know that's not really me and it's *not* going to involve making her sick, but this is happening."

"Good." Caroline grinned, eyes lighting up. "I'll help."

"Eliot?"

Mattie and Caroline looked at Eliot, but Eliot pretended to be extremely interested in the meadow around them.

"How's this going to work anyway?" Caroline asked, studying the cemetery. It was still creepy, still thick with weeds, and aside from them, very empty. "Do we just leave the food for the clones or what?"

Mattie didn't want to leave the burgers. Ants could get into them, or animals could steal them. Maybe they could just wait around and one of the clones would show? It wasn't like they didn't have a ton of raking and weeding to do anyway.

Then again, he did have a lot of pent-up anger from Delia. Mattie stomped to the edge of the woods and bellowed, "Doyle? You in there? Hey, Doyle! DOYLE!"

At first there was nothing. Well, there was a very confused set of Spencers. Caroline and Eliot watched Mattie and wondered if he'd finally lost his mind. But then there was a crack. There was a rustle. Then came the stomp, and Doyle wandered out of the trees, hands poised like he was carrying a tray. "Why are you yelling?"

Mattie shrugged, feeling a little embarrassed but at the same time somehow oddly calm, because a good round of screaming can do that for a person. "I didn't know how else to find you," he said at last.

"Oh." Doyle paused. "Well, you're lucky because it's baking time. I have to pick up sugar, you know. We're out. It's super annoying."

"Uh, yeah." Mattie nodded. "I hate it when that happens too."

"Totally," Caroline added.

"Bonkers," Eliot muttered, but everyone ignored him.

Doyle carefully put down his invisible tray on top of a headstone. "I can't believe you came back!"

"We said we would." Mattie tugged the two fortified burgers from under his sweater and offered them to Doyle.

The clone carefully wiped his hands on an invisible towel and took the burgers. "Yeah, but people say a lot of things. Hey"—Doyle looked over his shoulder—"Maxwell? Let's go!"

The leaves shivered and a branch cracked and Maxwell appeared. Mattie wouldn't have thought it possible but he was even dirtier than Doyle. The clone's navy pants were mostly brown. His hair stood up in stiff spikes.

Mattie peered a little closer. He had no idea what made Maxwell's hair stand up like that and he was pretty sure he didn't want to know.

Maxwell pointed a stick at Mattie. The end was disturbingly sharp. "Who goes there?" he demanded.

Doyle leaned over and thumped Maxwell twice. The other clone's head spun around. When it finally faced forward, Maxwell grinned at them. "Hello! Who are you?"

Doyle sighed. "Sorry. He stands in the rain too much."

"Uh, okay." Mattie edged forward and passed Maxwell a vitamin burger. "We brought you something to eat."

Maxwell flicked his spear stick to the ground and grabbed

the burger. Mattie and the Spencers leaned against a headstone to watch them dig in. Usually the clones were tidy eaters. They used silverware. They wiped their mouths. Not so much anymore, Mattie noticed, but they did chew exactly eight times.

Maybe they're not too damaged, Mattie thought.

"This is great!" Doyle said, slurping vitamin burger juice off his fingers.

"It's something," Caroline muttered. "I'm not sure I'd call it great."

Mattie nodded. Then again, Doyle had been eating invisible muffins and Carter's leftovers for the past few months, so almost anything had to be delicious at this point.

"Glad you like them," Mattie said, a chilly breeze whipping his hair around. Maxwell burped loudly and thumped his chest.

"Gross." Eliot waved one hand in front of his face. "I can smell it."

The only thing Mattie could smell was rain, but when he looked up, the sky above the cemetery was still bright blue.

Weird, Mattie thought as that same chilly breeze swirled through the woods again. Moments before, it had been so still. Now the wind was cranking up.

"Mattie?" Caroline asked slowly. "Do you hear something? It sounds almost like a train?"

She glanced toward the sky and looked past Mattie. Her jaw dropped.

"What is it?" Mattie turned and stared. Snaking through the graveyard was a long, thin dark funnel.

"Is that a cloud?" Eliot asked.

Mattie went cold. "No! That's a tornado!"

WHEN IN DOUBT, RUN FOR IT

"IT CAN'T BE," MATTIE BREATHED.

But it was. The tornado snaked toward them, picking up speed. It sucked in a bench, a bush, and the wing off a headstone's gargoyle. The wing spun into the air and crashed onto the ground. Bits of stone sprayed everywhere.

Mattie's eyes bugged. "Run!"

And they did. The clones dashed into the woods. The Spencers ran for the school and Mattie followed. They rushed through the crooked gate, going as fast as they could across the grass. Leaves whipped past Mattie's cheeks, catching on his clothes before being sucked behind him.

"Hurry, Mattie!" Caroline was five strides ahead, now six. "C'mon!"

Mattie ran faster, huffing and puffing with every stride.

"You're going to get sucked up!" she shrieked.

"I can't go any faster! I'm *short*!"

"That's no excuse!" Caroline returned as she leaped over a fallen tree branch and powered up the hill.

Mattie galloped after her. Faster. Faster. His lungs squeezed tighter. He glanced behind him and . . . there was nothing. The trees had stopped shaking. The leaves had returned to the ground.

The tornado was gone.

"Look!" he yelled, slowing. But the Spencers did not stop and they did not look. They were running hard for the school. Mattie flung himself forward, just barely catching Eliot's sleeve and hauling him around. "*Look*," Mattie repeated.

This time, the Spencers stopped and looked. They'd reached the formerly-overgrown-courtyard-now-turned-tidy-courtyard and Mattie tumbled into the grass, gasping. After a moment, he heaved himself onto his back and stared up at the sky. It was a bright, clear blue. No clouds. No wind. Nothing to hint at what had just happened.

"That—that—that!" Caroline's fury made Mattie sit up. She was staring at him, tight-lipped and pale, and for once, her hair really was windswept. Bits of leaves were caught in the curls and Caroline's dark eyes were wild. "That was a tornado!"

"Yes," Mattie managed, still heaving for breath.

"A *tornado!*"

"*Yes!*" Mattie was sitting down, but his knees were still shaky. That is the thing about adrenaline. It is great to get you away from snakes, tornadoes, and Tupperware parties, but eventually you're left with wobbly legs and a desperate need to pee.

"First, clones! Now, *tornadoes?*" Eliot brushed off his clothes, but it did little good. There were grass stains on his knees and some sort of smear on his sleeve. Eliot examined it closely, sniffed it, and made a disgusted face. "This school is going to be the end of me!"

Mattie agreed and scratched away the tickling between his shoulder blades. He glanced around, feeling like someone was watching them, but the courtyard was deserted and there was nowhere to hide. The hedges had been trimmed and the grass had been mowed—even the ants were now gone. The stone angel was still there too, but someone had smeared a creepy clown lipstick smile on her. Mattie shuddered as she stared at him.

"Guys," Mattie began. "This is like when we had the thunderstorm in the science room."

"Yep," Caroline said, eyes still huge.

"And it's like that storm during the photo shoot," Mattie continued.

"Yep," Eliot said, eyes also huge.

Mattie stared at the Spencers and waited and waited. His

friends heaved a sigh. "I see your point," Eliot added. "But even if it's true, no one is ever going to believe us."

Mattie nodded—and then stopped. Eliot was right: no one would believe them. "Except, when it started raining in History, Lem didn't exactly seemed surprised."

"What?" the Spencers asked.

"Lem. In history class. He didn't seem all that surprised by the rain. He seemed more nervous. Didn't you notice?"

Eliot shook his head.

"I was a little busy trying not to get electrocuted," Caroline said.

"Well, I don't think he was surprised—and when you consider the other things Lem isn't surprised by . . ." Mattie trailed off, thinking about chipmunk-munching moss and acid desk dissolvers. The Spencers' eyes widened like they were thinking the same thing too. "Maybe he's been experimenting with other stuff?"

"Like weather?" Caroline crossed her arms and glared in the direction they'd come. "No one likes bad weather. Who would want to make a thunderstorm?"

"I don't know." Mattie shrugged. "It's as good an explanation as anything though. What if Lem or Dr. Hoo or one of the other scientists is behind it?"

The Spencers went quiet. "Could be," Eliot said at last, brushing off his jacket sleeve again. "Or, like, Headmaster Rooney has gone from cloning us to trying to kill us."

His sister shook her head. "The Rooster wouldn't be behind this."

"How do you know?"

"He's way too perky. This is pretty scary stuff."

"I don't know," Eliot said, rubbing one hand through his blond hair. "Like I said before, raining ceilings isn't really creepy or scary. It's more—"

"Pointless?"

Eliot nodded. "Why would anyone want to make it rain indoors? I mean, yeah, it's bad for the furniture or whatever, but we got out of class. It's kind of a good thing."

In many ways, Eliot was right, but Mattie shook his head. "This is Munchem, remember? They never do anything small around here and whatever they plan it's never *ever* good."

Eliot nodded. "Well, at least that's the one thing you can count on."

"What do you mean?" Caroline asked.

"At Munchem, nothing stays secret for long and it always gets worse."

IT CAN ALWAYS GET WORSE, BUT SOMETIMES IT GETS BETTER . . . AND SOMETIMES IT GETS EVEN WORSE THAN WORSE

YES, INDEED, ELIOT WAS RIGHT: THINGS *CAN* ALWAYS GET WORSE.
This is a good thing to keep in mind especially when dealing with your own life and especially, *especially* when dealing with anything at Munchem Academy.

But even if you aren't dealing with Munchem, it still applies. You broke your leg? Well, you could've broken your neck. You forgot the code to unlock a bank's supersecret security system? Well, you could've . . . Actually, no that's really bad and would probably get you caught by the police.

In fact, Eliot Spencer's experience at Munchem Academy is probably what led him to believe escape plans are always—*always*—worth the effort and life is too short not to get the computer you want.

But Mattie and the Spencers weren't thinking about any of those principles as they made their way to the cafeteria for lunch. The friends turned at a stone bust of Mr. Larimore and walked down a set of stairs lined with paint cans and hammers. Munchem's renovation was still going strong and someone—probably Doyle—was going to find those and use them. Mattie didn't know exactly what Doyle would use hammers and paint for, but he was sure the discovery wouldn't go well for anyone.

"We have to tell Carter," Mattie said as Olga Higgins stared him down. "He'll know what to do."

"Like what?" Eliot asked.

"Dunno. That's why I'm going to ask him."

Mattie and the Spencers followed some fifth graders through the heavy double doors and into the high-ceilinged cafeteria. It was crowded as ever and they had to wait for the upperclassmen to finish picking out their food.

Last term, Munchem meals were closely supervised by teachers. Mattie was always careful to select healthy food and he was even more careful to make sure the teachers saw him selecting healthy food. This term, the scientists-turned-teachers didn't seem to care what the students ate. They just wanted to see the students' reactions.

Salads were replaced with pills, chicken nuggets were now streamlined for "even faster eating!," and the ice cream was fortified with sixty-two "necessary nutrients." Only no one seemed to know what those nutrients were or why one of them (or perhaps all of them) made a few of the students burp bubbles for days.

It did make the scientists very excited though.

Mattie considered his plate of freeze-dried and vitamin-charged hamburger. There hadn't been any problems with it before, but there was always a first time. He pushed his way through the crowd to join Eliot and Caroline at the closest table. Dr. Hoo and Lem stood along the far walls, watching the kids with careful interest and holding tiny voice recorders close to their mouths as they whispered observations.

Eliot surveyed his lunch as Mattie sat down next to him. "I can't decide if Munchem food has gotten better or worse."

"Definitely worse," Caroline said, impaling a round brown ball with her fork and holding it up for closer inspection. "I don't even know what this is."

"Maybe that's for the best." Eliot took a big bite and thought about it for a moment. "It's chewy—like the rubber they make Barbie doll legs out of."

Caroline groaned. "I hate Barbie dolls. They set impossible expectations."

"Totally," Eliot continued, still chewing. "I mean, heads do not come off that easily in real life. Seriously."

Caroline ignored him and turned back to Mattie. "Are you going to find Carter?"

"Yeah." Mattie stood on tiptoe and looked over the crowd.

There was Maxwell. There was Doyle about to spit on Maxwell. There was Lem shaking his pocket recorder.

Oh. There's Carter, Mattie thought. His brother was two tables away, nodding and smiling at an eighth-grade girl. She had pale hair and long, thin fingers tipped in hot pink. Mattie had never seen his brother agree with someone so much.

She must be fascinating, Mattie thought as he walked closer. He tapped his brother on the arm. "We have to talk."

Last term, Carter would've ignored him, but now his brother heaved to his feet. Carter jerked his head for Mattie to follow him. They retreated to a deserted corner of the cafeteria and Carter leaned one shoulder against the wall.

He took a big bite of his apple. "Okay. Talk," he said, chewing.

"Something's going on. First, we had a thunderstorm in History—like, *in* History. It was inside our classroom."

Carter stopped chewing. "What?"

Mattie repeated everything, and this time, added, "I think someone's experimenting with Munchem's weather."

"Why?"

"I don't know. Maybe it's an experiment gone wrong. Maybe it's an experiment gone *right*! Who knows? It's bad though. We could've died in that tornado and the clones are still out there and someone could find out what we did last term."

Carter's eyebrows pushed even higher and Mattie took a breath. "We have to do something," he said finally. Carter took another bite of apple. He chewed slowly.

Mattie leaned closer. "We were almost electrocuted in the thunderstorm and the tornado tore a wing off a stone angel. Think what it could've done to us!"

"I don't know what you want me to do. It's not your problem. Let it go."

"It is our problem! Dad isn't here to stop it, so *we* have to! The company could get blamed."

Carter shrugged. "Would serve him right. Look, Mattie, Dad thinks I'm horrible."

Mattie wilted. "You're not."

"I know that. You know that. But Dad doesn't—and if he thinks I'm horrible, fine. I'm going to *be* horrible. I'm going to take care of me."

Mattie had never felt so small. "You're not going to help, are you?"

"Nope. Business is busy, and I have things to do."

"Things like feeding the clones I hope."

Carter waved one hand. "Yes, *jeez*. Look, Mattie, you want help becoming who you are? I'm all there. You want to save Dad? You're on your own."

And then Carter walked back to his table and Mattie really was alone. Slowly, Mattie made his way back to the Spencers and flopped into his seat.

"Carter doesn't want to help."

Caroline frowned. "Surprise, surprise."

"What now?" Eliot asked.

The three friends stared at one another. No one could think of why you would create tornadoes. No one could think of how Larimore Corporation could use them. And even more importantly, no one could think of how any of the Larimore scientists would create tornadoes in the first place.

Unless . . . Mattie shook himself. He took a deep breath, forcing himself to say: "What if someone did something to the machine?"

Eliot paled. "The"—he dropped his voice—"the *cloning* machine?"

"Is there any other machine I should know about?"

"No! Impossible!" Eliot paused. He was thinking hard and Mattie knew this because thinking hard always made the skin between Eliot's eyebrows pleat and his mouth scrunch up. "Well . . ." Eliot said at last.

"Exactly."

They all looked at one another. Caroline sighed. "You know what that means?"

"What?" Eliot asked.

Mattie frowned. "We have to check the basement."

NEVER RETURN TO THE SCENE
OF YOUR CRIME

WELCOME TO MUNCHEM ACADEMY'S INFAMOUS BASEMENT. WELL, NOT the infamous basement—not yet—but welcome to the meadow that leads to the trapdoor that leads to the ladder that leads to the steps that lead to the basement. Confused? So was Mattie.

"I know the door is around here somewhere," he muttered, peering closely at the grass. It was a good night for sneaking around. It wasn't too cold or too hot and the bitten-in-half moon cast just enough light across the meadow so Mattie didn't stumble. Well, he didn't stumble much.

"Oof!" Mattie rubbed his shin. By this point, he'd run into a nest of field mice, a long black snake looking for the field mice, and now an old tree stump hidden by the spiky overgrown grass.

"Maybe we've gone too far?" Caroline asked.

"No way." Mattie ran his hands through the long tufts of grass. It sent clouds of gnats into the air. Some of them drifted past Mattie. The rest headed for his eyes and nose. Mattie sneezed and then sneezed again. "The door has to be somewhere close."

The Spencers agreed. In fact, the three had been looking for the trapdoor for the better part of twenty minutes now. This was the trouble with hidden doors. They didn't want to be found.

Or one of the troubles. The others were gnats and overgrown weeds with thorns.

"You don't think the repair team could have buried it or something?" Caroline asked, grimacing down at her thornpricked thumb. "Like, destroyed it during some of the renovations?"

Mattie gulped. He hadn't thought of that. "Do you remember seeing any of the workers over here? Any of the bulldozers or cranes?"

The Spencers shook their heads. "But that doesn't mean it didn't happen," Caroline said.

"You're very cheery," Mattie told her.

Caroline smiled. "I try. You know we don't have much time," she added.

Another cheery observation, but it was also true. Mattie kicked at a bit of rock, thinking everything over. "We could go in through Rooney's closet," he suggested. They'd accidentally discovered the basement's other entrance last year while hiding from the teachers and looking for a book possibly called the *How to Be Good Manual* (long story). Hidden behind coats, the small door led straight down to the basement and the basement's cloning machine.

"No way," Caroline said, attention straying back toward Munchem. Most of the windows were dark, but orange light still escaped the gym's new skylights. The scientists were working late. "If we break into Rooney's office again, we'll get caught for sure."

Again with the cheery, but Mattie had to agree. "There is that."

He sat back on his heels and considered the meadow. It was a perfectly good meadow with lots of grass and lots of flowers, but because it was also a Munchem meadow the grass was filled with prickers and the flowers made Mattie break into hives.

Mattie stood and brushed off his pants. Maybe they were too far to the west. Maybe if they tried going—

Clunk.

Mattie's sneaker caught on something and he pitched face-first into the grass. Milkweed went up his nose. Mattie rolled over, rubbed his now stinging elbows, and tried not to sneeze. "Found it."

Mattie pushed to his feet and Eliot and Caroline helped

him pull up the metal cover, revealing a narrow ladder leading down into an equally narrow tunnel. Small lights flickered and flickered and finally caught, illuminating the ladder's metal rungs.

Eliot cleared his throat. "Is it just me or does it look darker than it did last year?"

It wasn't just Eliot. Mattie agreed. Even with the lights, the narrow tunnel looked forbidding, like somewhere you would stick someone so you could take his fortune for yourself.

"How much do you really want to check the basement?" Eliot asked.

Mattie lifted his chin. "A lot. If they're planning to do something to us again, we have to know."

He scooted closer to the tunnel's opening and swung one leg down, feeling for the first ladder rung with his foot. Mattie looked at his friends. "Are you coming?"

"Of course," Caroline said, following right behind him.

And down they went.

Down . . . and down . . . and *down* . . . and . . .

"I forgot how long this ladder was," Mattie muttered. Above him, the Spencers grunted. Eventually Mattie's feet hit steps and, after an equally interminable time descending those steps, they reached the basement.

Or, rather the door that led into the basement. It was slightly ajar. Mattie peeked through the sliver of space between the door and jamb.

"What do you see?" Eliot whispered.

"Nothing." Which wasn't precisely true. Mattie saw pipes, power lines, two smokestacks, and row after row of black-screened computers. The generators were still near the wall. The electrical panels were still closed up tight, and there wasn't a single scientist in sight—and no clones either, which was a bit of a relief actually.

Mattie took a deep breath, smelling machine oil and cold concrete. He nudged the door open so they could creep inside. The ceiling was as cavernous as Mattie remembered, so high and so shadowy it looked like it was made from darkness. And the machine? The machine was even bigger than Mattie remembered. It spread from wall to wall in a tangle of computer bits and electrical parts.

"No one's here," Mattie whispered. For some reason he couldn't bring himself to lift his voice. Maybe it was because the basement brought back so many memories.

Had it only been five months since Mattie and the Spencers had discovered the cloning machine in the basement? Only five months since Carter had chased them down here and gotten stuck and had to turn himself in to Headmaster Rooney in order to save Mattie?

It sounded rather complicated when put like that.

Mattie looked at the Spencers. Everything seemed complicated these days. He sighed and turned to the huge computer screen and equally huge keyboard. Mattie studied the red buttons. There were the usual numbers and letters, but also strange symbols and fractions. "Who needs an eleven and two-tenths button?" he wondered.

"Same people who need personal tornadoes," Eliot said.

"No one *needs* personal tornadoes," Caroline told her brother.

"I do. I *need* a personal tornado—and I still want a clone."

"You're impossible," Caroline retorted.

"And you're—"

"Has the machine been modified?" Mattie interrupted before the Spencers could get going. "Can you tell if anyone's used it?"

Eliot stared at the closest keyboard like it was everything he'd ever wanted. His fingers twitched.

"Go ahead and touch it," Mattie said with a sigh. Eliot flung himself into the black desk chair, and the computer screen brightened, revealing a row of files and programs. Eliot began to open them. For several moments, there was only the sound of Eliot's fingers flying fast and sure over the keyboard. Caroline and Mattie glanced at each other and then glanced around them. There was something spooky about being in that dimly lit basement again, something that made Mattie's skin crawl like it was covered in spiders. Even Beezus seemed to agree. The fat, molting rat scurried under Caroline's sweater again.

"I want to check the wiring," Eliot said, ducking underneath the computer desk. His butt wiggled from side to side until he disappeared entirely behind a blinking electrical panel.

Caroline gave Beezus a scratch. "If the tornadoes aren't coming from here, where do we look next?"

"I don't know."

"There's nothing here," Eliot said, popping up from under the tangle of piping. He had dust on his nose, chin, and shirt. The rest of Munchem might be clean, but the basement was as dirty as ever. "It's the same machine."

For the first time ever, Eliot sounded disappointed in the cloning machine. It was a dead end. They were no closer to discovering what was really going on than they were before.

"We better get going," Mattie said, trying to keep the disappointment out of his voice.

"Five more minutes?" Eliot asked, eyes huge and hopeful.

"NO!" Mattie and Caroline yelled. Eliot grumbled, but he followed Mattie and his sister to the steps, and the three went up, up, up, which was far more tiring than going down, down, down. Mattie didn't mind it too much though. It gave him plenty of time to consider tornadoes and cloning machines and how an elevator would have been a much smarter investment for the Munchem basement.

Eventually Mattie did reach the very top. He pushed the trapdoor aside and peeked around the meadow. He saw weeds, weeds, and more weeds. Mattie pulled himself onto the grass and leaned back down to help Caroline. She grabbed his hand and he heaved her up; then they both pulled Eliot.

Caroline tugged so hard Eliot fell on his face. "Sorry about that," she said.

"No, you're not."

"Yeah, you're right."

Mattie and Caroline dragged the trapdoor back into place while Eliot kept watch. "We good?" he asked.

Mattie nodded, and the Spencers followed him up the hill and toward Munchem. What a disaster, Mattie thought. No leads on the tornadoes. No ideas where to look next.

Eliot rammed his shoulder into Caroline's and she staggered sideways. "You jerk!" she hissed and shoved him.

Mattie sighed.

At least we aren't going to get caught, he thought.

And that was when he saw the shadow moving toward them.

THERE ARE ALWAYS PEOPLE WHO
ARE WORSE THAN YOU

THERE IT WAS AGAIN: THAT PRICKLING ON MATTIE'S SKIN, THAT
spray of goose bumps between his shoulder blades, and just
like before, *there* was that itching in his teeth. Of course, this
time, Mattie was too scared to scratch it. He was too scared
to move *period*.

Mattie stared and stared into the dark. Maybe it was the
wind in the trees. Maybe the branches were shifting in the
moonlight.

Maybe you're seeing things, Mattie thought. But he wasn't,
because the shadow kept coming. It darted between flowering
trees and manicured bushes and cold sweat popped up between
Mattie's shoulder blades. It wasn't just shadows. It was a *person*.
Someone else was out here.

Mattie shuddered as the shadow glided on. It's not rushing toward us, Mattie thought. It's going somewhere though—fast too.

Everyone stayed still as they watched the shadow creep along very . . . well . . . creepily. Caroline leaned close to Mattie's ear. "Is it a student?"

Mattie shook his head. "I can't tell," he whispered. "A teacher?"

Caroline shifted. Mattie was pretty sure she was shrugging. "Maybe, but why be so quiet if it's a teacher?"

And Caroline was right (again) because the shadow person was being very quiet. Just as quiet as Mattie and the Spencers were being. It didn't want to be caught either.

They watched the shadow creep closer to the school. It paused under one of the windows and looked up. It stared for several seconds.

"Guys?" Caroline whispered. "Isn't that your dorm?"

Mattie craned his head to look. It was. The shadowy person was looking up at 14A's second window—looking up at 14A's second window like he or she was thinking about breaking in! Mattie held his breath, and after his very own personal forever, the shadow turned and moonlight caught its shiny blond hair.

"Delia," Mattie breathed. "It's Delia."

Indeed it was. Delia stood beneath their dorm window for another agonizing moment before disappearing back into the shadows.

"What's she doing out here?" Caroline whispered. "Why's she sneaking around?"

The clouds slid away from the moon and Mattie could see the Spencers again. Eliot's eyes were round and Caroline's mouth was open.

"What do you think she's looking for?" Eliot whispered.

"Us?" Mattie guessed. "The clones?" The idea made his heart double thump. The clones! Was Delia heading for the woods?

"C'mon." Mattie motioned for the Spencers to follow as he trailed behind Delia, sticking close to the wall and deep in the dark. They crept along and crept along and *finally* reached the tidy patch of grass by the gym. Mattie huddled by a marble statue of Mr. Larimore, and the Spencers hid next to the rosebushes.

If Delia's sneaking into the woods, she's going the wrong way, Mattie thought. There was a bark of laughter from above, and he glanced up. On the second floor, uneven windows cast yellow light across the stone trim and mossy gargoyles. There was nothing—*no one*—here.

Did we pass her? Did we— Mattie froze as moonlight slithered over something white. It moved along the gym's wall. Mattie squinted. It wasn't Delia. It was one of the scientists.

But which one? The scientist paused, the moon dipping him (her?) in silver and black, and as Mattie and the Spencers watched, Delia tiptoed out of the dark, careful to avoid the security cameras perched on the gym's gargoyles.

"What are they doing?" Eliot whispered.

Mattie shook his head. "Dunno. Too far away to hear."

They were also too far away to see. Moonlight caught the scientist's white lab coat and Delia's pale hair, but not much more. Delia and the scientist talked briefly, and then went in opposite directions. Two more heartbeats, and they both vanished completely into the night.

Mattie slumped down. "Pretty sure that wasn't a question about homework."

Caroline shrugged, her tangled hair even darker than the dark. "I bet she's after the clones. Just because you wouldn't help her doesn't mean she's going to stop searching."

Mattie frowned. It was a perfectly reasonable assumption, but it didn't feel like the full answer and he couldn't explain why. In later years, Mattie would call this "trusting my gut," but right now it just seemed like something was plucking at him, something that didn't have a name. Yet.

"This isn't good," Caroline continued, hugging both arms around Beezus. The rat's eyes bulged. "This soooo isn't good. One of the scientists is helping her."

Eliot nudged Mattie with his elbow. "You know, I recognize the hypocrisy when I say this, but your dad really needs to upgrade the security around here."

"He had to take the cameras down! Professor Shelley told him hackers could look through the cameras to spy on our technology and . . ." Mattie trailed off, skin going cold. "What if Delia was meeting with Professor Shelley? She would know exactly where they could meet to avoid the security cameras. *Plus*, she's into robots. She had a whole lab full of them back at the Larimore Corporation. What if she told my dad the security system should be taken down?"

In the moonlight, Caroline's downturned mouth turned into a slash. "But why would she do that?"

Mattie paused. "I don't know. I *do* know she sided with Delia even though you two swore I had nothing to do with the glitter, and she was also involved with the security system being taken down, so that's something, right?"

Slowly, the Spencers nodded. Everyone looked at the shadowy spot where Delia had met the mystery scientist. "What if," Mattie continued, "Professor Shelley didn't advise my dad to take down the security cameras because she wanted to keep people from spying on Munchem? What if she had him take them down because she wants to keep what she's doing a secret?"

NEVER EAT YELLOW SNOW

MATTIE DIDN'T SLEEP MUCH THAT NIGHT. HE TOSSED. HE TURNED.
He was about to flop on his stomach again when Eliot kicked him from below.

"You're shaking the whole bunk," Eliot whispered. "Knock it off!"

Mattie did, but he still couldn't sleep, and by the time the alarm went off Mattie's eyes felt gritty and his legs felt ten times heavier.

Across the room, Doyle bounded out of bed. "Going to be a great day!" he said with a maniacal gleam in his eyes.

Probably means he's plotting something with Delia, Mattie thought as he dragged himself into his clothes. It was even more disturbing when Mattie considered Professor Shelley might be helping.

Everyone dressed in silence, and just before Doyle banged out 14A's door, he pointed finger guns at Mattie. "Be seein' you, Little Larimore."

Yippee, Mattie thought. He stared at Kent's empty bunk for a long moment. The dorm felt extra quiet without the other boys. Until now, Mattie didn't realize silence could have weight. "Eliot?" he asked at last.

"Yeah?"

"I want to see what's inside the gym."

"And I want to see what's inside the clones."

Mattie sighed. "I'm not kidding."

"Neither am I," Eliot said.

Mattie sighed again. "The only thing still protected at Munchem is the gym. Whatever's in there must be pretty amazing."

Eliot tucked his Munchem T-shirt into his pants. "Yeah," he admitted.

"If Shelley's involved, it's probably a computer." Mattie paused. "Wouldn't you want to see it?"

Eliot looked at him, eyes narrowed. "Well played, Little Larimore."

"Shut up. I'm serious."

"I am too."

The boys looked at each other as the late bell began to

chime. Mattie trudged after Eliot. It was a quiet breakfast. Caroline spent most of it passing food to Beezus while the boys stared into space. Everyone picked at their food, and no one said anything on the way to class.

In fact, it seemed like it was going to be just another day at Munchem—until Mattie pushed through the doors to see clouds swirl over the morning sun. The lovely spring morning suddenly turned dim and the sky went dark as wet concrete.

"It's going to rain," Caroline said.

A cold, cold wind nudged under their clothes. Mattie shivered. "I don't think that's rain."

And, as the friends watched, neon yellow snow began to fall from the sky.

All the students stopped and all the students stared. It wasn't that snow is unusual at Munchem. The academy was known for blizzards that will freeze your pipes and your eyeballs. Icicles would form on the gargoyles that were so thick and sharp they could be used as weapons—the absolutely most perfect weapon too, because the icicle will melt away after you stab someone with it. So, yes, in short, snow was not unusual at Munchem.

But it never snowed anything *yellow*.

"Ohgross-ohgross-gross-gross-gross!" Caroline danced in a circle as she banged pee-colored snowflakes off her sweater. Mattie agreed, but apparently Eliot did not.

He opened his mouth and caught a fat flake on his tongue. "Looks like snow," Eliot said. "Tastes like snow."

Caroline gagged.

"Look!" Doyle shouted and ran past them. He spun in circles on the lawn, arms outstretched like he belonged in a musical with lederhosen and hills that were alive. "It's snowing!"

Something heavy plowed into Mattie. It was Maxwell, galloping to join Doyle. A dozen Munchem students followed him. Everyone danced around, shrieking and laughing.

Everyone except for Caroline and Mattie, that is.

And Lem.

Just like when the thunderstorm erupted, Lem didn't seem surprised. He caught a single snowflake on the tip of his finger and pulled out his pocket recorder. He muttered something into it. Lem was calm. Lem was thoughtful. It lasted two heartbeats before he announced very loudly, "What a strange storm! It must be from global warming!"

The Spencers and Mattie exchanged a glance. "Is it just me or does Lem seem to be trying a little too hard?" Mattie asked.

Caroline nodded. "Totally. He's being even weirder than usual."

"Yellow snow falling from the sky is a good reason to be weird."

"True."

Eliot licked another snowflake off his finger. "Delia's going to be bummed she missed this."

Caroline and Mattie ignored him. They dusted snow out of their hair and off their shoulders and—

What's that? Mattie wondered. He paused, mid dusting. The gym's frosted-glass windows were a dusky, flickering pink. *Like something's burning.*

Mattie looked from the yellow snow on the ground to the pink-illuminated windows on the gym, and his teeth began to itch. Mattie elbowed Eliot. "Still don't want to take a look inside the gym?"

"What do you mean?" Caroline asked.

"Look," Mattie whispered. The Spencers followed his gaze, shoulders tightening when they saw the bright windows.

A slow grin spread across Eliot's face. "When do you want to go?"

Mattie glanced around. Half the school was running outside to see the yellow snow, and the rest were already here. The students were laughing and the scientists were muttering to each other and *everyone* was staring at the sky. No one was paying any attention to Mattie and the Spencers.

"C'mon!" Mattie said. For the briefest of moments, the Spencers were confused. Then they realized what he was doing.

"I like the way you think," Eliot muttered, racing after his friend. While the students and professors ran back and forth, Mattie and the Spencers skirted the edge of Munchem's walls. While Lem shouted about acid rain turning into yellow snow, they slipped up the steps. While everyone stared at the still-dim sky, the three friends used a back hallway to circle toward the sophomore foreign language classes.

But instead of turning left, they turned right, and there it was: a sole, shiny wooden door—a sole, shiny wooden door with pink light peeking around its edges. Outside, yellow snow came down harder.

Mattie's mouth went dry. This is it, he thought, taking a step. This is—

The door wiggled as someone shook the handle and opened the lock.

"Get down!" Caroline whispered, grabbing Mattie and Eliot by the back of their sweaters and hauling them into the nearest open classroom. They crouched by a row of metal desks as the door opened and relocked. Mattie leaned forward, holding his breath. Footsteps grew closer and closer.

Professor Shelley hurried past.

She had an armful of papers and a troubled expression and didn't notice Mattie at all. Which was an excellent thing since Mattie didn't have an explanation for why he was hiding in a classroom, but he did have an explanation for why Professor Shelley was leaving the ballroom-turned-gym.

"I'm telling you," Mattie whispered to the Spencers as the footsteps disappeared and they were alone again. "Shelley's behind this."

"But why?" Caroline crouched against a desk. "If she's behind everything, why hasn't she taken *all* the cameras down?"

Mattie thought about this. He shrugged. "Villains move in mysterious ways."

"Maybe." Caroline still didn't look convinced. "I mean, if weird weather is the goal, she got it—yellow snow is weird— but I don't think Professor Shelley looked happy. She seemed scared."

NO PEEKING

IT WAS THE LONGEST—AND COLDEST—WEEK OF MATTIE'S LIFE, AND when the yellow snow finally melted, Mattie packed as many superfood corndogs under his sweater as he could and headed for the cemetery with Caroline and Eliot right behind him.

"These things are gross," Eliot complained as they trudged through the cemetery gate, boots crunching across half-frozen grass. "My stomach's all greasy now. The clones better appreciate this." He held up a foil-wrapped corndog and peered at it. "What makes this a superfood anyway?"

"I'm not sure I want to know," Caroline said, pulling out her own corndogs and arranging them on the top of a head-stone.

Mattie started to agree, and felt something tremble beneath

his feet. He paused, and felt the tremble again. "What was that?"

Deep, deep, deep in the woods, something pink flashed. "Did you see that?" Mattie whispered.

"Oh, yeah," Eliot said.

Caroline nodded. "What do you think it was?"

Mattie watched the shadows. The pink flashed again. The ground trembled again. "Something's up. Something worse than before."

"Do you think it's the clones?" Caroline asked. "Could they be in trouble? Malfunctioning or something?"

Mattie's stomach twisted hard. They could be. If rain made their eyes malfunction, what could the snow have done?

Another pop of pink lit up the branches. Mattie threw down his rake. "C'mon."

Mattie waved the Spencers into the woods as he watched the cemetery and fields behind them. Munchem sat up on the hill, and as the afternoon sun slid behind it, the school looked bigger and darker than ever.

"Hurry up, Mattie!" Caroline said.

Mattie ducked after them. They pushed deeper into the woods. This far in, it smelled like wet earth and pine needles. The thick canopy of leaves blocked out most of the afternoon sunlight and Mattie concentrated on his feet so he didn't trip.

"Hey."

Mattie and Eliot turned around. Caroline had stopped

walking. She stared up into the trees with both arms wrapped around Beezus.

"What is it?" Mattie asked.

"Did you notice how quiet it's gotten?"

Mattie hadn't, but now that Caroline mentioned it, the woods *were* quiet. There weren't any birds calling or any squirrels chattering. Nothing rustled in the leaves and nothing flew past them. It felt almost as if the entire forest was holding its breath.

"Not just quiet," Eliot said and swallowed. "Too quiet."

Beezus squeaked as if he quite agreed, and *that* was when they heard the first explosion. It split a nearby tree, hurling it to the ground. Branches and twigs flew everywhere, and a particularly hard acorn thunked Mattie in the head.

He ducked. "Get down!"

The Spencers were already down. They pressed their faces into the piney forest floor and felt bits of tree fly past them. A minute passed . . . then another. The woods had gone quiet again.

Mattie peeked through his fingers. "It's okay, I think." He pushed to his knees and looked around. A cool breeze wound through his hair. Mattie shook himself and pine needles went everywhere. "What was that?"

Eliot helped his sister up. They were both trembling. "No idea," Eliot said, picking leaves off his shirt. "It was like someone set off a bomb. The tree just exploded."

"Trees don't explode," Caroline said as she tried to detach Beezus from her hair. The rat clutched her frizzy braid with two tiny paws. His whiskers twitched frantically. "Something happened."

The breeze picked up, bringing a wave of pollen with it—and the sound of voices. Mattie tensed. "Do you hear that?" he whispered.

Caroline and Eliot nodded. "Do you think it's the clones?" Caroline whispered.

Mattie shook his head. The voices were too deep and there were too many of them to be Doyle and Maxwell. "They sound like grown-ups," he whispered. "Maybe teachers?"

"Why would the teachers be out here?"

Mattie stood. "Let's find out."

"Are you *crazy*?" the Spencers hissed.

Maybe a little bit at this point. For anyone keeping track, this is the second time this semester Mattie has hit his head—well, okay, *technically*, the acorn hit Mattie—but the point is, head injuries often make you think you have a good idea.

Even when you don't.

Like right now for instance, when Mattie crawled to the top of a rise and peered down into the hollow below them. What he saw should have made him scramble back the way he'd come. It should have made his stomach go cold and slushy—actually, it still made his stomach go cold and slushy—but Mattie didn't move, and whether that had to do with his head injuries or the fact that this was another step toward his future of thievery, we will never know. What we do know is Mattie saw Dr. Hoo in the forest clearing.

He was muttering to himself and standing next to a machine. What kind of a machine? Mattie couldn't tell. It had a wide base that narrowed into a point like a triangle. A string of green lights ran down both sides. A wide keyboard covered the front. And as Mattie watched, the machine began to tremble and shake and then its fat belly slowly turned traffic-light red.

Mattie leaned forward. "What do you think it's doing?"

Lightning shot from the top. It arced across the clearing.

Boom!

Another tree exploded. It crashed to the ground and someone screamed. Mattie was pretty sure it was Eliot. Mattie covered his head with both arms as pine needles and twigs showered down.

"Another bull's-eye!" Dr. Hoo cheered.

He's talking to himself, Mattie realized. *That can't be good.* Mattie lay with his cheek pressed against the ground and listened as Dr. Hoo went on and on about the importance of trajectories and never giving up on his dreams.

"What is he *doing*?" Caroline whispered furiously. Beezus was now clutching her throat, making her whisper especially wheezy.

"How am I supposed to know?" Mattie whispered back.

"It's not like I can ask him. We're not supposed to be out here."

"We need to leave!" Eliot lay behind Mattie. "Now!"

Mattie rolled over. He couldn't stop himself. It was just that, out of the three of them, he would've expected Eliot to want to stay—and try to take the machine apart.

Eliot narrowed his eyes like he knew exactly what Mattie was thinking. "Excuse me if I don't want to be crushed to death by trees!"

"Dr. Hoo," a voice boomed. Dr. Hoo *wasn't* alone! "If I wanted to hit trees, I'd talk to a lumberjack. Impress me. Show me how it's going to take down a person."

Mattie swallowed and felt his throat click. Take down a person? That sounded *horrible* and, as is often the case with horrible things, Mattie had to look. He had to see who had just said that. So, slowly, carefully, Mattie shifted back onto his stomach and wiggled through the dirt and pine needles so he could peek over the rise again.

Dr. Hoo was still standing by the lightning machine, but someone new had joined him. He was the tallest, broadest man Mattie had ever seen. His camouflage pants and shirt blended perfectly with the surrounding forest and his massive brown boots crushed everything they stomped on.

"Who's that?" Eliot asked. It seems Mattie wasn't the only person who couldn't look away when something horrible was happening.

Mattie shook his head. "No idea."

"He looks like he's in the army or something," Caroline added.

Mattie agreed. It wasn't just the man's uniform, there was something about the upright way he carried himself that made Mattie think he was in the military—and there was something about the way the man barked his orders that made Mattie think he wasn't just military, he was an officer.

Dr. Hoo smoothed one hand over his springy brown hair. "General Mills, the Weather-matic 9000 isn't just a weather machine. It's a revolution."

The general crossed his arms. "Go on."

"Thanks to its advanced crystal core, you can make any day a good weather day. Would you like to work on your tan in Iceland? The Weather-matic has a setting for that."

"I'm not interested in turning Iceland into Florida, Dr. Hoo. I'm interested in seeing that target taken out." The man pointed to an odd straw man propped up at the edge of the woods.

"But isn't it nice to have options?"

It *was* nice to have options. Mattie just wasn't sure they needed this one.

"The point is," Dr. Hoo continued, "you will finally control your day. No more rain—unless you want it. No more snow—unless you want it. No regular old clouds—unless you want it. Everything will be up to you—including colors and shapes!"

The yellow snow and the foot-shaped cloud . . . ?

"Why would I want colored rain?" the general asked.

And why would you want yellow snow? Mattie thought.

"Why wouldn't you?" Dr. Hoo beamed. "Again, my friend, it's all about options. Think how patriotic you would look at your next event if it rained red, white, and blue."

"It would still be rain."

"*Patriotic* rain."

The general frowned. He seemed to be considering it though. "How does it work anyway?"

Dr. Hoo's face lit up. "The Weather-matic depends upon its one-of-a-kind crystal core. Thanks to my highly specialized and highly advanced innovations, the crystal's powers have been harnessed to do our bidding."

"'To do our bidding'?" Eliot whispered. "Does this guy hear himself?"

Mattie thought about reminding Eliot of the time he had said the same thing and decided against it.

General Mills rocked back and forth on his feet. He didn't seem impressed with Dr. Hoo, but he couldn't take his eyes from the Weather-matic. "I thought your partner was supposed to join us," he said at last.

Dr. Hoo's eyes narrowed. "I don't have a partner anymore. She didn't keep her end of the bargain."

Mattie shivered. Dr. Hoo looked downright scary. General Mills, however, looked unimpressed. "And your boss?" he asked.

Hoo shrugged. "Larimore was called away. Trust me, he doesn't have a clue what's going on. It's the one thing my former partner did right."

"Good," General Mills said, resting both meaty hands on his belt. "Now show me the lightning bolt setting again."

Dr. Hoo flashed a salute, and scurried to the machine's side. He typed something on the keyboard. The Weather-matic 9000 began to shake. Its potbelly turned a pale pink and then red and then *darker* red and then . . .

Boom!

KNOW WHEN TO SELL

A LIGHTNING BOLT FLASHED FROM THE WEATHER-MATIC'S TOP. IT arced in a jagged pink line over the men's heads and *whoosh* the straw man exploded. Bits of flaming pants fluttered to the ground and Dr. Hoo blasted them with a fire extinguisher.

"Amazing!" the general shouted.

Mattie agreed. There was nothing left of that straw man! Mattie's stomach gave a sickening little lurch. There was *nothing* left of that straw man!

Dr. Hoo smiled. "As you can see, your target will look as if he or she was the victim of an unfortunate lightning strike. No one will ever know it was intentional."

Now the general was smiling. He shook his fist. "Again!"

"Gladly." Dr. Hoo typed out another sequence on the keyboard and the Weather-matic began to shake and shiver. Seconds later, pink lightning cut across the clearing and another straw man went up in flames. The general clapped his hands in delight.

"That is so cool," Eliot whispered. Mattie agreed, but he also still felt a bit sick. The general had wanted to know how the machine would take down a person and now he knew. He wasn't interested in sunny days or beach vacations. He wanted to use the Weather-matic as a weapon.

Mattie looked at Caroline. She was very pale and probably thinking the same thing Mattie was, because her eyes were very, very wide.

"Again! Again!" The general jumped up and down. His heavy boots thumped hard against the ground. "Do it again!"

Dr. Hoo began to type, but before he even finished the Weather-matic started to turn red again. "Uh-oh," Dr. Hoo said, backing away.

Uh-oh? Mattie strained for a better look. *Why is Dr. Hoo—*

Pink lightning shot in all directions from the top of the Weather-matic. It hit the last straw man. It hit the underbrush. It hit the tree on Mattie's right.

"Duck!" he hissed and all three of them curled into the dirt as pine needles and twigs and a bird's nest littered the ground.

"Uh, we seem to have some technical difficulties," Dr. Hoo continued and Mattie could hear something smacking the Weather-matic's metal side as, presumably, Dr. Hoo whacked it.

Mattie squeaked opened his eyes and glanced around. Branches littered the forest floor. They were lucky nothing heavy had fallen on them!

"Whoops!" Dr. Hoo cried and more lightning lit up the clearing. *Whack! Whack! Clang!*

Dr. Hoo was hitting the Weather-matic. Branches were falling to the ground. And the general? Well, the general was grinning.

"I'll take a hundred of them!" he shouted. "How soon can you have them ready?"

"Well," Dr. Hoo began, "I'll need to develop another crystal core first. The original took almost a month. It's very complicated, you see, but if I use the current crystal as a jumping off point for more crystals, it shouldn't take as long, but I have to get it right or I could damage the Weather-matic and— look out!"

More lightning hit the treetops and Mattie scurried backward. "Go!"

All three of them wriggled away on their bellies. They scuttled past fallen trees and underbrush and a particularly dazed-looking squirrel. In fact, Mattie didn't stop wriggling until he could see the mausoleum's roof peeking through the tree line and he knew the Weather-matic and Dr. Hoo were far, far behind them.

"Hold on!" Mattie sat up and brushed dirt off his chest. "I have to catch my breath!"

Caroline and Eliot stopped and everyone looked at each other.

"Just when I think things can't get any weirder at Munchem," Caroline said, shaking her head.

"Weird?" Eliot's mouth hung open. "We nearly died at the hands of a Larimore Corporation death ray!"

"It isn't a death—" Actually, it would make a great death ray. Mattie's eyes bugged. "Holy crap! It's a death ray!"

Beezus squeaked, but if that was in agreement, Mattie couldn't tell.

"And they *swore* Wrinkles Away was an accident," Eliot added. "I bet it wasn't. I bet it was an elaborate way to assassinate their enemies. That's exactly what evil scientists do." He paused. "I wonder if he'll use the cream on his former partner. Would be a good way to get rid of something. Not as good as a death ray, of course, but—"

"Who do you think his partner is? Was?" Mattie asked.

Caroline shrugged. "Hoo said 'she.' Could be anyone."

"Or it could be Professor Shelley," Mattie said. "She's behind Munchem security—or the *lack* of Munchem security."

"Well," Eliot said at last, rubbing a bit of dirt from his

cheek. It was getting dark and Mattie couldn't tell if Eliot had actually cleaned it off. "You were right about the weather, Mattie."

"Yeah," Caroline added. "They just weren't using the cloning machine to do it."

Mattie shrugged. Usually, being told you were right is a good moment, but right now it didn't feel good at all because yes, Mattie was right about the weird weather, but there wasn't any satisfaction to it because that weird weather was going to be used for blowing people up.

"What are we going to do?" Mattie asked.

"You keep asking that and I keep telling you: nothing." Eliot stood and helped Caroline to her feet. Mattie didn't move.

"We *can't*, Mattie," Eliot continued. "You said it yourself, this is *Munchem* and we're *kids*."

"That doesn't mean we can't do the right thing!"

"C'mon, Mattie," Caroline said. "We can't stay any longer. Someone's going to miss us." She hauled Mattie up by his arm and dragged him into the cemetery. Far up the hill, the sun was disappearing behind Munchem and it turned the school's three and a half towers into three and a half horns. Munchem was still as scary as ever.

"We have to do something," Mattie continued. "Dr. Hoo's already hurt people—think of Kent and Bell and Rooney. They're just the beginning if he sells the Weather-matic to that general!" He took a deep breath. "Someone has to tell my dad."

"Not it!" the Spencers said in unison.

Mattie narrowed his eyes. This wasn't the first time his friends had invoked Not It, and it wasn't the first time Mattie had been caught out by Not It.

"Don't look at us like that," Caroline said, stroking Beezus. Bits of rat fur took to the air and she waved them away. "You know the rules of Not It."

Mattie did indeed. What he didn't know is why he always forgot to say Not It before Caroline and Eliot did.

"Besides," Caroline added, "your dad's going to want to know why you were down here. How are you going to tell him without giving away Maxwell and Doyle? They're kind of Larimore Corporation inventions too. How can you protect them?"

"I don't know," Mattie said miserably. "But I can't *not* say anything. It's wrong."

"It's wrong to get the clones in trouble too."

Mattie nodded. Caroline was right. Doing the right thing almost felt like doing the wrong thing and Mattie didn't know what to think about that. "We can't stay quiet."

"Well, technically . . ." Eliot paused and exchanged a careful look with Caroline, one Mattie understood well. Technically, they *could* stay quiet. They didn't have to say anything. They could pretend to know nothing. His dad described it as "keeping your head down." Mr. Larimore said it was a good thing—especially around attorneys and people who worked with income taxes.

But Mattie didn't think he could stay quiet. This was a dangerous invention. People could get hurt. In the wrong hands, people *would* get hurt.

And Mattie would know he could have stopped it. "I won't keep this a secret. My dad has to know."

TIMING IS EVERYTHING

OF COURSE, THE PROBLEM WITH MATTIE DOING THE RIGHT THING AND telling his dad and outing Dr. Hoo for being an evil scientist was the fact that Mr. Larimore wasn't actually at Munchem. He was still away on business. Mattie was going to have to call him, which brought up another problem because the students weren't allowed to use the school's phones.

"Everyone's going to be heading for dinner," Mattie whispered to the Spencers as they made their way up through the dead gardens and into Munchem. "If you could create some small distraction to keep it that way, I can slip into Rooney's office and call my dad."

Caroline petted Beezus through her sweater, and Eliot chewed his thumbnail.

"So you're going to do something wrong to do something right?" he asked at last.

"Pretty much."

"Okay, so long as we're all on the same page."

Mattie ignored him and took a left toward the administration wing. The overhead lights had been dimmed and Mattie's shoes tapped quietly against the hardwood floors. At the hallway's end was the headmaster's door.

Mattie glanced around. No one. He rapped lightly on the door. No response.

Now or never, Mattie thought, and he took a few deep breaths for courage, but it only filled his nose with dinner smells and did nothing to lessen the tightness around his ribs. *Please don't let me get caught.* Please *don't let me get caught.*

And Mattie reached for the doorknob. It turned easily, silently, maybe even a little eagerly in his hand. It was at that moment that Mattie wondered why the office hadn't been locked. Because someone trusted the students? (Ha!) Because someone forgot? (Possibly.)

Or because someone was coming back?

Mattie's armpits went swampy. He needed to hurry. Just like in the hallway, the office's lights were low, pooling shadows in all the corners and under all the furniture. Mattie rushed to the big wooden desk and picked up the phone. He dialed his dad's cell phone number and waited for the line to connect.

Click. Mattie hesitated, peering at the phone's receiver. There wasn't a ring, and even when the call went straight to voice mail, his dad's voice mail usually had a greeting, not a click. Then again, the line hummed as if it had connected. Maybe it *is* working, Mattie thought.

"Dad!" Mattie faced the desk and curled over the phone so he could keep his voice down. "We have to talk! Dr. Hoo has given a weather machine a lightning setting and it can kill people! He's going to sell it to the—"

"Ahem."

Mattie's blood turned to slush. Slowly, he turned, spotting Dr. Hoo and Delia only a few feet away. Delia was smirking her nasty smirk, and Dr. Hoo was twirling the end of what looked like a telephone cord.

Mattie peered closer. *That's because it* is *a telephone cord*, he realized.

"I told you he was in here," Delia said, teeth glinting in the low light.

Dr. Hoo took a step toward Mattie, and—

Wham! Wham! Wham! Wham! Footsteps crashed down the hallway and Carter burst through the office door. Panting, Carter looked from Mattie to Hoo to Delia. "Uh, hey, um, there you are, Mattie. I've been looking for you everywhere! We have that thing we have to do."

Mattie dropped the phone. "Oh, yeah, that's right. I forgot."

Carter nodded frantically, dark hair flopping across

his forehead. "Exactly. That thing with lots of other *adults*."

"They're expecting me," Mattie explained as he edged around Dr. Hoo and Delia.

"Oh, I bet they are," the scientist said, sounding as if he didn't bet it at all. "You'd better run along."

Delia's face flushed a deep purple. "Aren't you going to do anything?"

"Quiet," Hoo hissed. "I'll deal with it."

The hair on the back of Mattie's neck stood up. "Yeah, uh, I better, you know, go—"

Carter caught his arm and dragged Mattie toward the hallway as Delia swore under her breath. She was focused on Mattie getting away, Carter was focused on Mattie getting away, and Mattie? Well, Mattie couldn't help himself. He glanced back. Dr. Hoo smiled at him.

And then Dr. Hoo drew one finger across his throat.

———

In later years, Mattie would say he had never felt so helpless and so scared. Dr. Hoo was an adult. He was an evil genius. And he was out to get Mattie—who was currently trying to keep up with his brother, who was dragging him somewhere. Mattie wasn't sure where. He couldn't focus. He didn't know what to do. He didn't know what to say. He didn't know what to *think*—even if he could think. Panic had turned his brain staticky or maybe it was just that his head was filled with *Dr. Hooisouttogetme!*

"This is sooo not good," Mattie said to himself.

"Ya think?" Carter stomped down the administration hallway and turned for the dorms.

They'd just gone down the first flight of steps when Eliot caught up with them. "Hoo and Delia weren't at dinner!" Eliot whispered.

"Yeah, I figured that out," Mattie said. "How did you know to save me?"

"I saw them follow you into the office. Mandy and I were down the hall. We were, uh, busy," Carter said.

"Doing what?"

Carter gave his little brother a jerk. "You're killing me, you know that? What did I say?"

Mattie sighed heavily. "That I should pretend I don't know anything."

"And what did you do?" Carter asked.

Mattie sighed even more heavily. "Tried to tell Dad everything I knew and now Dr. Hoo knows I know and he just dragged a finger across his throat like he was cutting my head off."

Carter said some of Mr. Larimore's favorite curse words, and behind them, Eliot whistled in admiration.

"Seriously?" Mattie asked.

"What?" Eliot shrugged. "It's impressive."

"I can tell you what else is impressive," Carter said darkly, stopping at the corner so he could better glare at Mattie. "Captain Do Right's ability to—"

"I can't do this right now," Mattie said and kept going. Eliot and Carter tore after him, but Mattie didn't stop. A floor above, the hallway leading to 14A smelled like vanilla cupcakes, but even the scent of sugary deliciousness couldn't improve Mattie's mood. He couldn't stop picturing how Dr. Hoo had drawn a finger across his throat.

The boys stomped through 14A's doorway, and Mattie flung himself facedown on Eliot's bed. For once, he was glad Kent and Bell hadn't returned to school after the mudslide. Mattie could have his nervous breakdown in private.

"Hoo's going to kill me and make it look like a lightning strike." The sheets smelled like Thanksgiving turkey. Mattie wrinkled his nose and rolled back over. "I'm a dead man."

Eliot sat on the bed's edge, studying his hands, the walls, the floor—basically anything that wasn't Mattie.

Mattie sat up. "Eliot?"

"Yeah?"

"This is the part where you tell me it won't happen."

"I can't. It's totally going to happen."

"Hey," Carter said, patting Mattie's shoulder. Mattie looked hopefully at him. Maybe his brother would know what to do. Maybe his brother could make him feel better.

"Eliot's right," Carter said and then flicked Mattie's ear as hard as he could. "What have I always told you?"

"Ow!" Mattie rubbed his ear. "To kick Doyle in the crotch if he tries to stick me in the toilet again."

Carter flicked him again. "*No*, what's the other thing I always tell you?"

"To shut up?"

"Exactly. It applies to so many situations. It's like the Golden Rule."

Mattie thought about explaining (again) to Carter about what the Golden Rule really was, but his ear hurt too much. He flopped back on the bed and contemplated the top bunk's cracked underside.

"My point is, you shouldn't have told Dad," Carter continued.

"I had to. Think of what would happen to anyone General Mills doesn't like! Think of what could happen to Dad!"

"So *that's* really what this is about." Carter tried to flick him again and Mattie twisted away. "You're worried about making Dad look good. Did it ever occur to you, Mattie, that maybe he deserves to be embarrassed? He hired those homicidal maniacs. They're his fault."

Mattie glared at Carter. Carter glared at Mattie. "That's not what it's really about,'" Mattie said at last. "It's just another reason I had to do something."

"Well, now *you're* going to die, so yay you."

"Do you think people smell like barbecue when they've been hit by lightning?" Eliot asked, swinging his legs back and forth. "Or do you think they smell like burned chicken?"

Mattie groaned. "I don't want to think about it. Going up against Hoo is like being in a horror movie."

"What?" Eliot and Carter asked.

"You know how in scary movies the bad guy always outsmarts the hero until the very end?"

Carter laughed. "You think you're a hero?"

Mattie glared at him. "No. I'm just using it as an example. The bad guys always think of everything. They cover their tracks. They cut the good guys off from help. That's how they get away with being bad."

The boys thought about this. All three looked very serious. Mattie looked, perhaps, more serious than Eliot or Carter, but the prospect of being barbecued can do that to a person.

"Mattie?" Eliot asked at last.

"Yeah?"

"If the bad guys always get away, maybe you should start thinking like one of them."

"How am I supposed to think like a bad guy?" Mattie asked. He sounded a little horrified, and that was appropriate since we all know Mattie is supposed to be the only good kid at Munchem. He should sound horrified. He should *be* horrified.

But Mattie kind of sort of wasn't, because Eliot's words

had given Mattie an idea—an idea so good that a smile broke across his face. He looked at Eliot and Carter and Eliot and Carter started to look a little worried.

"What?" Eliot asked.

"Guys," Mattie said. "I know how I can stop Dr. Hoo. He said the Weather-matic's crystal core is one of a kind. So, we steal it."

MATTIE LARIMORE'S EVEN BIGGER BOOK OF BAD

LIVE UP TO YOUR POTENTIAL

WELCOME TO ANOTHER IMPORTANT MOMENT IN MATTIE'S EVOLUTION.
Most biographers don't include it because they lack attention
to detail—and by "most biographers" I actually mean Alistair
Wicket, who probably writes his drafts in crayon.

Thankfully, however, I have loads of details to pick from,
including how Carter will eventually set fire to Dr. Hoo's car
and Mattie will put it out, but that's for a later date and has
no place here because right now we're concentrating on how
Eliot's eyebrows had just shot halfway up his forehead and
how Carter was wiping away happy tears from his eyes.

"Steal the crystal core?" Carter echoed, smiling a big, happy
smile and patting his now damp cheeks. "I never thought I'd
hear you say something like that."

"It's the fastest way to stop Dr. Hoo." Mattie jumped to his feet and began to pace. "Think about it. Dr. Hoo said the crystal core is the only one of its kind. He needs it to make more. No crystal. No Weather-matic 9000."

Eliot's eyes went wide. "That's a great idea!"

Carter shook his head. "Except for the part where the Weather-matic is impossible to get to."

"Which is why they'll bring it to us."

His brother sighed as if Mattie had given him a massive headache. "Yeah, that's not how being a bad kid works, Mattie. People don't give stuff to you."

"Shut it. I'm not being bad. I'm stopping *Dr. Hoo* from being bad—from being *awful*. Think how many people he could hurt by selling the Weather-matic!" Mattie paused. To pull this off, he would need something big, something unexpected, something that would really light a fire under Dr. Hoo and the other scientists.

Wait. Mattie tensed. A fire?! He snapped his fingers. "We'll get them to bring the Weather-matic out of the gym by setting the gym on fire."

Carter froze. "Do go on. I'm all ears."

Mattie opened his mouth and closed it. He loved his brother. He loved how Carter treated him like a friend now, and he especially loved how Carter no longer called him dog names, but Mattie wasn't sure he loved the gleam in Carter's eyes.

"No," Mattie said finally. "Hold on. Not a fire. That's too dangerous. We just need something that will make them think the inventions are at a bigger risk for staying in the gym versus coming out of the gym. We need them to *think* there's a fire."

Carter's smile fell and he blew out an enormous, long-suffering sigh. Perhaps he *was* long-suffering. After all, no one at Munchem enjoyed random acts of arson quite as much as Carter Larimore. "You disappoint me, you know that?"

Mattie ignored his brother. "What about the ventilation system?" he asked Eliot. "My dad bought a new one. It's supposed to be controlled by one master computer system. Could you overload it or something?"

Eliot shrugged. "Probably. If I could, it would get the alarms to go off. They might start evacuating everyone. I would just need a way into the system—maybe through the wireless, but they'd be stupid not to have it secured and—"

"You're overthinking it. You don't need any of . . ." Carter made a face. "Any of what you were just talking about. You just need a way to clog the vent system."

"Well, then we need something to clog it with." Mattie studied his brother. "Carter? What do you have?"

"Nothing," Carter said quickly.

Too quickly, Mattie thought. "Without me, you'd still be in that cloning pod under the cemetery."

His brother sighed another long-suffering sigh. "Fine. I don't technically *have* them, but I can get about two thousand crickets. I was saving them for just this sort of emergency."

Mattie and Eliot gaped.

"You were *expecting* something like the Weather-matic?" Eliot asked at last.

"No, I was expecting my math midterm, but I can get them, and you can use them, and I'll come up with something else for Algebra."

"How do we know this will work?"

Carter snorted. "It's me. Of course it will work."

Mattie and Eliot stared at him and Carter rolled his eyes. "Who put the dead possum in the air-conditioning unit last term?"

Mattie tried not to gag at the memory. He'd been in Mrs. Hitchcock's class, trying to figure out how to get out of Munchem, when they'd smelled the dead possum. Carter had stuffed it into the vent so every time the air turned on, the class was buffeted by stench. People had vomited. Mrs. Hitchcock had fainted. It had been awful and also rather epic.

Carter smiled to himself, eyes misty as if he were recalling that day too. "I enjoy using the school's infrastructure against the teachers."

And that was true, Carter certainly did, but Mattie was more impressed his brother knew the word "infrastructure," which is supposed to refer to a building's skeleton, but for Carter it was an opportunity for mayhem.

"Anyway," Carter continued, "we can dump the crickets

into the air vent on the south wall—they still haven't cleared away those rosebushes, so we'll have cover—and then we wait. The crickets will prevent the air from moving properly plus they stink. And they stink even more when they die, so there's that."

It wasn't a bad idea. Mattie thought it over. Nope, it definitely had potential. Except . . . "I don't think stink is going to make them evacuate the inventions."

"Yeah," Carter admitted. "It's just a nice add-on. They'll evacuate the inventions when the crickets start falling through the ductwork and into the new heater Dad had installed. Remember when he showed us the plans?"

Mattie didn't, actually, because whenever Mr. Larimore pulled out Munchem's building plans, Mattie tended to zone out. In fact, the only thing Mattie remembered from their discussion about kitchen improvements was "blah blah blah Mattie blah blah blah."

Carter sighed. "He gives you an excellent opportunity like that and you don't pay attention?"

"I didn't realize it was a great opportunity."

His brother loosed another sigh. "When the crickets hit the heater, they'll start to burn." Carter spoke very slowly. "Burning equals smoke. Smoke equals sensors going off. Sensors go off? The alarms will sound. It's foolproof."

Mattie wasn't so sure about foolproof, but he liked the idea. "Okay," he said finally. "Let's do it. We'll have to be fast though, before Hoo starts making more crystals. When can you get the crickets?"

Carter made a face. "Couple of days? Depends on how quickly the clones get to the tackle shop."

Mattie started to nod, and stopped. "The clones you're *feeding*, right?"

Carter heaved a tremendous sigh. "Yes, the clones I'm *feeding*. We good?"

They were not even the farthest thing from good, but Mattie shrugged. "Yeah."

Carter stretched his arms above his head. "Now who wants fortified fish fingers? You better eat while you can, Mattie."

Mattie's stomach churned. Some of this was due to the fact that Dr. Hoo was out to get him and fortified fish fingers might be his last meal, but more of it was due to anticipation. Whenever Mattie was about to pull off a plan, he lost his appetite. In later years, he would know this was just part of who he was, like having brown eyes and a soap-opera-actress mother. Then again, there was always the fact that fortified fish fingers never sounded particularly good. Even so, he followed Eliot and Carter out of the dorm and down the stairs.

"Hey, Mattie," Eliot said when they reached the bottom step.

"Yeah?"

"For someone who can't think like a bad guy, you came up with the idea to steal the crystal core awfully fast."

"It's thanks to me," Carter told him. "I'm a great role model." Carter thought for a moment, one corner of his mouth turned up in concentration. "To pull this off, we're going to need a distraction."

Mattie nodded. "Yep."

"So we need an idea."

"Nope," Mattie said. "We just need Caroline."

LEARNING YOUR CRAFT STARTS AT HOME

"IT'S TRUE," CAROLINE SAID THE NEXT MORNING. "THEY ALWAYS need me. It's because I'm usually right about everything."

Carter rolled his eyes, but he didn't argue, and for that, Mattie was grateful. Caroline had missed breakfast, and after some searching, they'd found her in the Student Laboratory—a very official-sounding name for a converted sunroom that smelled like cheese.

Or maybe that was just Doyle. Mattie's roommate was two tables over, snickering with Maxwell. Being around the bigger kid was always risky. Toilet swirlies, noogies, being spit on—in many ways Doyle's imagination was limitless—but now that he'd joined forces with Delia, Mattie was even more nervous around him.

"What are you doing anyway?" Mattie asked Caroline.

She looked down at the cluttered table. It was covered in dead computer parts. "Detention. I asked Delia if she used Elmer's Glue or rubber glue to style her hair. She told on me. Now I have to do an extra questionnaire for Professor Shelley's new toy."

Caroline held up an electrical board of some sort. It didn't look like a toy at all. It had sharp edges and a rusty middle. "Do you think this would be fun for all ages?"

Mattie thought for a moment. "It looks like something that would give you tetanus."

Caroline flipped the electrical board back onto the table. "I think so too. So what's the deal? What are we doing?"

Mattie glanced around. The Student Laboratory was never as full as Mr. Larimore had anticipated. Some of that might have been due to the cheese smell. More often it was due to the fact that Munchem students didn't really care about discovering things. They were more interested in stealing, lying, and making the scientists-turned-teachers cry.

"We need to get the Weather-matic out of the gym," Mattie told Caroline. "And to do that we have to get close to the air-conditioning units."

Caroline tapped her pencil against her lower lip. "Why the air conditioner?"

"We're going to overheat it. It will set off the fire alarm and the inventions will be evacuated."

"Oh. Good idea—wait." Caroline's expression turned suspicious. "How are you going to overheat it?"

"Well, you know how these things go." Carter scratched the back of his head until his dark hair stood up in spikes. "We'll put crickets in the air vent and let nature take its course."

"Crickets?" Caroline whispered, face flushing purple. "That's horrible!"

"But effective."

"You're disgusting."

Carter smiled. "Thank you."

Caroline clenched her pencil as if she were thinking about stabbing him. She faced Mattie instead. "What about the gym's security cameras? They're still active."

"That's why we're asking you—maybe we could throw something at them? Is there a way to block the lenses?"

Carter made a scoffing noise. "That won't work."

Caroline nodded. "I agree with the cricket killer."

"Hey!"

"I said I *agreed* with you." She twirled her pen around her fingers and Carter eyed it nervously. "Honestly. So touchy. Eliot?"

Her brother tensed. "What?"

"Remember when the Castevets got that security system to keep you away from their electric sports car?"

Eliot frowned. "I remember it differently."

"How can you remember sneaking into their garage

repeatedly to play with the car's wiring any *differently* than how it was?"

"Whatever. What's your point?"

"Didn't you do something to their security system? You made it sick or something?"

Eliot's eye roll was almost as impressive as his sister's. "I overloaded the operating system. It thought it had a virus and shut down. Honestly, if they'd wanted to keep me out, they should've tried harder."

"No doubt," Caroline said. "Could you do it again?"

Eliot frowned. "Of course I could. What do I look like? An Apple genius?"

Caroline paused as if she were thinking exactly about what her brother looked like, but she declined to share. She turned to Mattie. "If Eliot shuts down the gym's security cameras, you could get to the air-conditioning unit without anyone seeing you."

Mattie perked up. "How long would it be down?"

Eliot thought. "Either twenty minutes or permanently. It could go either way really."

Mattie went quiet. You could fit quite a lot in "twenty minutes or permanently." You could fit things like "That would be perfect," "That isn't long enough," and "I let my best friend hack into my father's security system." Mattie particularly didn't like the last one.

"Actually." Eliot paused, studying the other students like

they held answers. Sunlight streamed through the huge banks of windows, making the students look like they belonged in a boarding school for good children. "It could *not* go down at all too. There's always that."

Mattie glared at him. "I thought you said you could do this."

"I can! I think. I'm almost positive. Just, you know, look for the green light to shut off."

"It's a *red* light," Mattie said.

Eliot waved one hand. "You say tomato. I say potato."

Mattie chewed his thumbnail. Eliot made the whole thing sound easy, which considering Mattie would be the one sabotaging the air-conditioning unit and Eliot would be the one sitting in the attic with Marilyn, it probably did look awfully easy to him.

"Anything else that could happen?" Mattie whispered to Eliot.

"No." Eliot shook his head. "It'll either go down for twenty minutes, it'll go down permanently, or it won't go down at all. Those are your options."

Some options, Mattie thought. "How do we know there aren't cameras inside the gym?" he asked as the other students cheered. "There could be a layer of security we don't know about."

"What about a disguise?" Caroline asked.

Mattie eyed her. "What kind of disguise?"

She shrugged. "I don't know. Something good. Something they would never suspect you in."

Mattie started to say he had no idea what that would be and stopped. Twelve years living with Carter Larimore had taught Mattie a lot of things: how Play-Doh ripped out nose hairs when stuffed up your nostrils, how you should never *ever* sniff Carter's finger, and how, sometimes, the best hiding spots were the most obvious ones.

"I need to look like everyone else," Mattie said, straightening. The Spencers and Carter stared at him as if he were nuts. "Think about it: there are so many of us. If I look like a generic student, they'll never be able to tell which one of us it is."

"Not bad." Carter actually sounded impressed. He rubbed his chin, thinking. "But I'd take it one step further."

"What do you mean?"

Carter's eyes gleamed. "Use Doyle's baseball jersey. His name's on the back. If the cameras record you, they'll think he was behind it."

"No way," Caroline said, shaking her head so hard Beezus was slung side to side. "No one would ever confuse someone as short as Mattie with someone as huge as Doyle."

"Yeah, but that's the point," Mattie said eagerly. "Up close, no one would mistake us, but from a distance? If the security footage isn't that clear? If I have Doyle's shirt on, it'll confuse them."

"Until they look at your face," Caroline retorted.

Mattie thought for a beat. "I'll use his hat too. If I pull it down low enough, it could work."

"It'll at least give you some wiggle room if you *do* get caught," Carter added. He looked at his brother. "And if you do, remind the teachers this is America and you're innocent until proven guilty. And if that doesn't work, cry. Hard."

Mattie swallowed.

"Don't worry." Carter slapped him on the shoulder. "Dad would never expect *you* to screw up his expensive new vent system. You're the good son."

Mattie tried to smile. He was pretty sure his brother was being supportive, but it wasn't exactly working. There was a scuffle behind them, and Mattie looked up in time to see Dr. Hoo entering the Student Lab. His gaze swept the room, landed on Mattie, and stuck. Mattie turned his attention to the tabletop, but somehow he knew Hoo was still watching him. It made his scalp prickle.

"So are we doing this or what?" Carter whispered.

Mattie picked at his sweater, the uncomfortable feeling threading through him growing even bigger. That's the weird thing about emotions—they're never quite what you think they should be.

For example, anger feels big and round and like something you could chew on, but guilt? Guilt chews on *you* and, in the end, guilt will eat you alive. I like to think of it as the gift that just keeps on giving—like poison ivy or ringworm.

Anyway, the point is right now, Mattie felt guilty. He didn't want to damage the security system, but he didn't want Dr. Hoo to blast unsuspecting people into little bitty bits either.

Mattie took a deep breath. "Yeah," he said at last. "We're doing it."

The Student Lab door opened again, and Delia glided through. The sunlight caught behind her, turning her face into shadows and her body dark. It was only for a second though, and Delia was back to being Delia when she joined Doyle at his table.

"You know," Caroline muttered, suddenly becoming very interested in her would-be toy, "the cameras aren't your only problem. It's Delia's fault you're even on Dr. Hoo's radar. She's obsessed with taking you down. You need to do something about that. Distract her, or something."

Caroline was right. Mattie thought for a moment, and then turned to his brother. "What else do you have for sale?"

"Nothing really. Some powdered milk the clones thought I could use. No clue why."

Mattie perked up. "Powdered milk?"

"Yeah . . . why?"

Mattie smiled.

WHETHER IT'S SERVED COLD, HOT, OR WITH A SIDE OF BACON, REVENGE IS ALWAYS DELICIOUS

AN EVIL SCIENTIST, A DEADLY WEATHER MACHINE, AND FRIED CRICKETS? Frankly, it was a lot to take in—so much so, in fact, it would be entirely understandable if Mattie forgot about his promise to get revenge on Delia.

But he hadn't.

Not that Mattie revealed anything as they left Professor Shelley's class that afternoon. Eliot stayed behind to argue the merits of self-destructing viruses while Mattie and Caroline went on to American History. Ahead of them, Doyle and Maxwell shoved fifth and sixth graders aside so Delia could pass. Mattie could hear kids crashing into lockers as they walked down the hallway.

"I see Doyle and Maxwell have found their purpose," Carter

said, sliding between Mattie and Caroline. "Check it." Carter passed Mattie a handheld video game. "Business is good. Just got this one in for one of the seniors."

"We're not supposed to have those things," Mattie reminded him as they turned for the front of the school.

"Technically, I don't have it—only looks like the real thing. Serves that tool right."

Mattie tilted the handset back and forth. "It doesn't work?"

"Nope, but it doesn't matter. I'll tell him it worked fine for me."

"And he'll believe the lie?"

"If people believe it, it's not a lie."

Mattie followed Carter down the hall and out the heavy double doors into the sunshine. "That's not how lies work."

"Are you sure?"

"Positive."

"Well, whatever, I got your powdered milk too." Carter jammed one arm into his backpack and pulled out a tin can. He tossed it to Mattie. "Enjoy."

Oh, I will, Mattie thought. He followed Caroline down the stairs and to the right. To the casual observer, it looked as if they were taking the long way to American History. Mattie tried to walk along as if he were filled with thoughts on the Civil War rather than straining for one last glimpse of the gymnasium air vents he was about to fill with crickets, one last look at the—

"So what's the deal?" Caroline demanded.

Mattie blinked. "What's what deal?"

"Are you seriously not going to explain what you're doing with a can of powdered milk?"

"Oh." He glanced around. "Revenge."

Caroline brightened. "Do tell."

"Here." As they turned toward American History, Mattie popped the top off and waved the can under Caroline's nose. She gagged. "Exactly," he said, screwing the lid back on. "It's not pleasant, and you know what it would smell like if you rolled in it?"

Caroline pawed at her nose. "Like garbage."

"Worse." Mattie gave her a satisfied smile. "Delia will roll around in it and stink for days."

"How are you going to manage that?"

"I'm not. She's going to do it for me."

Caroline paused. "Go on."

"I'm going to sprinkle it in her sheets, and then when she goes to sleep, she'll roll around in it." Caroline still looked confused, so Mattie explained: "You sweat when you sleep. It'll get in her pores."

Her eyes bugged. "Remind me never to make you mad."

"I'm not just doing this for me. I'm doing this for *us*."

"And Beezus?" Caroline added.

Mattie sighed. He pocketed the can again. "And Beezus— but I'm doing it tonight and you're going to help."

Caroline was only too happy to help Mattie with his plan. In later years, she would go on record saying revenge was *not* a dish best served cold. It was best served hot and steamy and not really served so much as thrown in the person's face.

Unfortunately, however you decide to serve your revenge, there's always a period of waiting. Sometimes, you wait in a plushy lounge filled with leather chairs and sofas. Sometimes, you wait in a swamp filled with snakes and mosquitoes. And, sometimes, you wait in the perpetually broken girls' toilet with your knees drawn up so no one sees your dangling sneakers.

Which was exactly what Mattie had been doing for the past hour and a half.

His butt had gone numb by the time Caroline finally came to get him. She checked the other stalls to make sure they were alone and then tapped Mattie's stall door three times with her knuckles. "Everyone's gone downstairs for dinner," she whispered. "Now's your chance."

Mattie lowered his feet to the white tile floor and stretched his back. Hiding isn't so bad, he thought, but he only thought this because he hadn't spent two days stuck under an oil tycoon's desk yet. After that fiasco, Mattie wasn't a fan of hiding or people who liked to take their shoes off under their desks.

Caroline opened the bathroom door and stuck her head into the hallway. She motioned for Mattie to follow her. "Hurry up."

Mattie hurried, or rather, he tried to hurry. His knees kept popping like plastic bubble wrap and his feet had gone to sleep. It felt like his socks were stuffed with needles. He shuffled after Caroline.

She held open the door. "I'll keep watch."

"Good idea. Which bed is Delia's?"

"The bottom one in the corner."

Caroline's dorm was almost exactly like Mattie's. Bunk beds lined either side of the room and trunks sat next to each bed. Mattie's dorm had dirty brown carpet, but Caroline's had scarred wooden floors. Mattie's sneakers clattered against them.

"Could you *be* any louder?" Caroline asked without taking her eyes from the staircase.

Mattie stood next to Delia's bed and contemplated jumping up and down. It would indeed be louder and it would definitely irritate Caroline, but he had bigger things to accomplish right now. Mattie peeled back Delia's yellow striped covers and sprinkled powdered milk directly on the mattress. He studied the effects, then sprinkled some more.

And a bit more.

And . . . there. Mattie stood back. That was perfect. He tugged the sheets and covers back over the mattress and smoothed everything flat. It looked like it had never been touched. Mattie grinned. He dusted off his hands, leaving ghost prints across his sweater.

Drat, Mattie thought. He swiped at the powdery marks and made them worse. He brushed and banged and—whoops! The powdered milk can fell off the bed and hit the floor. It rolled underneath.

"Mattie?" Caroline sounded panicky by the doorway.

"One second." Mattie dropped to his knees and swept one hand under the bed. His fingertips bumped the can and it rolled farther under. Mattie groped around on the floor. He went left. He went right. He stuck his palm straight in a wad of used chewing gum.

Mattie gagged and yanked his hand back. The gum followed. Stuck to Mattie's skin, it stretched and stretched until he could see it wasn't gum at all. It was some sort of thin cable.

"Wha—?" Mattie managed just before there was a click and whirr and the bed lifted up a foot. Floorboards peeled back and a computer screen and keyboard lifted up. The keyboard swung toward Mattie's lap and the screen tilted forward and turned on. Blue static filled the screen and then suddenly snapped into focus.

Miss Maple's face filled the screen. "Why, Delia! I wasn't expecting you!"

VILLAINS NEVER TAKE VACATIONS

OH, NO! MATTIE SCRAMBLED BACKWARD. MISS MAPLE WAS AS ROUND and pillowy as ever. Her blond curls bounced and her smile was wide.

"How's my favorite niece?" she asked.

Mattie's blood went icy. *Niece? Miss Maple? DELIA?!*

Miss Maple continued to stare at him. She was waiting for Mattie to respond and Mattie had no idea what to say. His brain was stuck on things like: *There's a computer under Delia's bed* and *Miss Maple* and *WHAT THE HECK IS GOING ON HERE?*

"Mattie?" Caroline came around the edge of the bed and stopped dead. "What is this?" she hissed.

"Delia? What's going on?" Miss Maple peered closer at the

camera on her side. For a moment, the screen was filled with pink Miss Maple nose. "Is this thing on?"

The visual shook as if Miss Maple were tapping the camera. Mattie sat up. *She can't see me*, he realized.

Tentatively, Mattie waved, and just as he'd thought, the movement didn't seem to register with Miss Maple. The former school secretary just kept glaring at the camera.

"Stupid technology," she muttered, blond curls trembling. "I'll have the IT guy's head for this!"

"What's she talking about?" Caroline's eyes were as bugged as Beezus's as she knelt next to Mattie. "This is crazy." They looked from the keyboard to the floorboards to the computer screen. "Ugh, Eliot will love her even more if he sees this. Why would she even have it?"

"I think a better question is, why is Delia communicating with Miss Maple?"

Miss Maple peered closer again. "Is your keyboard not working, Delia?"

Keyboard? Mattie glanced down and spotted the keyboard again. "She can't see us and she can't hear us, so do you think Delia communicates with Miss Maple on the keyboard?"

Caroline shrugged. "Maybe? I don't know. Turn it off. We shouldn't be using it. Delia's going to know we were here."

"She's going to know someone was here anyway. Don't you think it's *more* suspicious if we just turn everything off?"

Mattie faced the screen, feeling something that might have been bravery filling up his chest. "I want to talk to her."

Caroline whimpered as Mattie reached for the keyboard. `Sorry for delay,` he typed. `Was thinking.` Mattie paused, fingers hovering over the keys. What would Delia be thinking about? `About Munchem,` he finished.

"I've been thinking about Munchem too," Miss Maple said. "I followed up on Lem and that Shelley woman. Trust me, if she wants to protect her job, she'll keep backing you up, but she better figure out how to get those gym cameras down. It can't be *that* complicated."

"Huh?" Caroline whispered. "Is that why Professor Shelley always sides with Delia and gives *us* detention?"

Mattie slowly nodded. It had to be. "*That's* what she gained by lying: protecting her job."

Caroline's face screwed up with confusion. "What?"

"My dad says—" Mattie started to explain, and couldn't. His voice locked inside his throat as Miss Maple leaned closer.

"Well?" the former secretary asked. "Aren't you going to say thank you? You won't have any trouble with those two!"

`Thank you!` Mattie typed. `That's really great.`

"That's 'really great'?" Caroline whispered.

"What am I supposed to say?" Mattie shot back.

"Well, you're welcome." Miss Maple smoothed a hand over her curls and Mattie realized Delia smoothed her hair the same way. How had he missed their resemblance?

"*What* is going on?" Caroline asked through clenched teeth. "I don't understand."

"I don't either," Mattie said.

"We should go." Caroline glanced nervously at the door. Mattie knew what she was thinking: they were taking too long.

"Five more minutes," Mattie whispered. "I have to know what they're doing. Help me sound Delia-like. How do I do that?"

Caroline looked as if she were weighing a number of different responses. Mattie turned to the computer. *What's new?* No, that wouldn't work. Or *How's it going?* Nope, definitely not.

Wait! Mattie sat up straight. `Do you have any updates?` he typed.

"Oh, yes!" Miss Maple peeked into the lens again. Her face curved into a mean little smile that looked *exactly* like Delia's mean little smile. "One of my contacts at General Mills's office reported today, and do you know what he told me? Hoo met with Mills. Without us."

Mattie's mouth hung open. "'Without us'? Miss Maple is Hoo's partner?"

Caroline tugged twice at the end of her ponytail. "Maybe? And that would mean Delia was meeting with Hoo, not Shelley, right?"

Mattie and Caroline stared at each other. Caroline tugged the end of her ponytail harder. "Why wouldn't Professor Shelley be able to get the gym security cameras down? She's the smartest person at Munchem. She would have to know how."

"Maybe she's stalling them, trying to protect the Weather-matic."

Miss Maple glowered into the lens. "Did you hear me, Delia? Hoo met with Mills."

She was expecting a response, but what were you supposed to say when you were pretending you just found out your scientist partner betrayed you? *I'm sorry?*

I'm sorry, Mattie typed.

"You should be!" Miss Maple's eyes went glazy and bright. "If you had found those last two clones, we wouldn't be in this mess. I promised Hoo those clones." Miss Maple sat back and smoothed her hair. "But," she continued, "if that fool thinks he can cross me, he can think again! All the security systems are still down." The mean little smile was back and Mattie and Caroline both shivered. "I'll come get that crystal myself."

THINK BIG PICTURE

THE CRYSTAL? MATTIE STARED. CAROLINE STARED. REALIZATIONS began to fall together: Dr. Hoo was going to sell the Weather-matic to General Mills, but Miss Maple was going to steal the crystal core before Hoo could sell the Weather-matic to General Mills, and Miss Maple was going to use the Weather-matic for . . .

Mattie gulped. "Wh—wh—do I say?" he whispered.

"'I'm looking forward to zapping people'?" Caroline suggested.

Mattie's stomach lurched like he might be sick. Caroline launched herself toward the computer and slapped the screen shut with so much force her hair shivered and Beezus squeaked.

"Caroline!" Mattie protested. "I wasn't finished!"

There was a soft whirring as it powered down. The screen and keyboard disappeared under the floorboards as the bed lowered.

Caroline grabbed Mattie's arm and hauled him to his feet. "Delia could be back any minute. Do you really want to explain what you've been up to?"

"I don't know. The powdered milk stuff really pales in comparison to stealing a high-powered weather weapon."

Caroline glared at him.

"It's true," Mattie said.

"You're killing me. Let's go."

They hurried to the door and Caroline cracked it open. She checked the hallway. "Okay, we're good."

"We are so not *good*," Mattie muttered.

They paused at the top of the steps, listening for anyone coming. Dinner was still going on, and a murmur of voices passed. Seconds later, it was quiet again. Even so, Mattie couldn't take a deep breath until they were down the stairs and headed for the Student Laboratory.

"I really wish Eliot had come," Mattie whispered.

"He would've wanted to smell her pillow."

"But he also would've wanted to help with the computer." Mattie paused. "No *wonder* she was so good in Professor Shelley's class."

Caroline grunted, but whether that was an agreement or not, Mattie couldn't tell. Considering it was Caroline and it was also Eliot and computers and Delia, Caroline's grunt could've meant anything.

They turned toward the Student Lab and spotted Dr. Hoo and Professor Shelley whispering at the end of the hallway. "C'mon," Caroline hissed. "They won't notice us."

Mattie did indeed "c'mon," but Hoo and Professor Shelley definitely noticed them. Professor Shelley didn't say anything, but Dr. Hoo flexed his hands like he was thinking about grabbing them. Caroline and Mattie surged forward, not slowing until they passed through the Student Lab's double doors.

Inside, Mattie dodged a couple of eighth graders and spotted Eliot sitting in the corner. They hurried toward Eliot, who flipped his book shut as Mattie and Caroline sat down. "So how'd it go?" he asked.

Caroline groaned. "I don't even know where to begin."

Eliot looked at Mattie and Mattie looked around the room. Lem was dozing in a patch of yellow light from the study lamps. Maxwell was carving stuff into the tabletops. Two sixth graders were flicking a paper football. And Doyle was staring at Mattie.

Mattie gulped. "Give me your book," he whispered. Eliot passed it to him and Mattie tried to explain as quietly as he could. He started with the generous application of powdered milk—while pointing at a set of math problems. He went on to whisper about how the powdered milk can rolled under the bed—while pointing at notes for the math problems. Then he came to the computer that connected to Miss Maple and how Miss Maple was planning to steal the Weather-matic's crystal core—and forgot to point at anything because retelling Eliot about it made Mattie break out in goose bumps.

"Miss Maple said Hoo wanted the clones and Delia never found them. But Miss Maple didn't care because the Weather-matic would soon be theirs. And *then* we panicked and shut everything down and came here." Mattie sat back. Eliot stared at him. His mouth hung a little open. Mattie didn't blame him. It was an awful lot to take in.

"You would really like Delia's setup," Mattie added. "It's hidden under her bed and you activate it by grabbing a lump of used chewing gum."

"Nice! Wait." Eliot frowned. "What happens if someone cleans under her bed?"

"She probably eats them for dinner." Caroline had been quiet through the whole explanation and now it didn't seem like she could be quiet for a moment longer. She faced her brother. "Delia's Miss Maple's *niece*!"

Eliot said nothing.

"Well?" Caroline demanded.

"Well, what?" Eliot asked. "What do you say to that?" He glanced at Mattie. "You know, it's pretty much your fault Hoo turned on them. You're the one who told the clones they didn't have to stick around to meet Miss Maple."

Mattie kicked his sneakers against the tile floor. "What are we going to do?"

"We could tell on her," Caroline suggested.

"Yeah, for the computer violation alone, she'd get thrown out of Munchem." Eliot did not sound nearly happy enough about this. Mattie and Caroline ignored him.

"I don't know," Mattie said at last. "Every time we try to catch her on something, she has an excuse. She plans for *everything*. I'm sure she has a plan for what to do if someone finds her computer."

Caroline made a face. "At least it would get her thrown out."

"But who cares?" The more Mattie thought about it, the tighter his chest got. "This is bigger than Munchem. Hoo could still replicate the crystal, and Miss Maple could still steal it. Horrible things are *still* going to happen."

Everyone fell silent because this was an excellent point. Why would it matter if Delia were thrown out of Munchem? It might make their lives easier for a time, but how long until Miss Maple and Delia took revenge by blasting them with lightning?

Blasting anyone they wanted with lightning, Mattie thought.

"No wonder Delia's so awful," Mattie added. "With an aunt like Miss Maple she's going to turn out to be an evil genius."

Eliot nodded. "That's usually how it happens in comic books—that and accidents."

"There's no such thing as evil geniuses," Caroline said.

"I don't know," Mattie said slowly. "In a school filled with bad kids, doesn't it seem statistically likely that at least one of us would grow up to be like Miss Maple or Dr. Hoo?"

Caroline still did not look convinced. "An evil *genius*?"

"We had clones last term," Mattie said flatly.

"Yeah, fair enough."

"Look." Mattie took a deep breath. "Maybe she's not a genius, but Delia and Miss Maple and Dr. Hoo are definitely using their powers for *evil* and we have to stop them."

Everyone fell silent again.

"So let me get this straight," Eliot said at last. "Dr. Hoo is selling the Weather-matic to General Mills. General Mills is going to use the Weather-matic to blow things up. Delia and Miss Maple are going to steal it before General Mills can get it from Dr. Hoo, and then *they* will probably blow things up."

Mattie thought about it. "Yeah, that's about right."

"Good grief, we have *really* stepped in it." Eliot passed a hand through his hair, making it stand up in wispy spikes. "How many bad guys can we have?"

Apparently, they had loads. It was worse than the movies. At least then bad guys looked like bad guys. As far as Mattie could tell, in real life, bad guys looked like everyone else.

Caroline shrugged. "We can do it. After all, there are five of us and four of them."

"Beezus doesn't count," Mattie said.

"Whatever. We can still do this."

Mattie thought Caroline sounded a bit like she was trying to convince herself, but he had enough sense not to say so.

"We just need the right opportunity," she continued.

"Are you thinking what I'm thinking?" her brother asked.

Caroline wrinkled her nose. "I hope not. I would hate to be trapped anywhere near your Delia-screwed-up brain."

Eliot held his response. Dr. Hoo had slipped into the Student Lab. His eyes instantly went to Mattie, and Mattie's eyes instantly dipped.

We're being watched, Mattie thought, rolling his hands into fists. He took a deep, *deep* breath. "Guys," Mattie whispered, pretending to be very, very interested in his lap. "We have to steal the crystal *now*."

BE PREPARED FOR
UNEXPECTED CONSEQUENCES

PUT LIKE THAT, IT SEEMED SO SIMPLE. MATTIE HAD THE RIGHT friends and the right plan and the right . . . underwear? Or, perhaps not. By the time Carter showed up with the crickets, Mattie had sweated through it.

Still, these things happened—usually only when Mattie stole a subway train, but apparently now it also applied to crickets and air-conditioning units.

Carter, however, did not look sweaty or nervous as he strolled up to meet Caroline and Mattie. They'd agreed to meet by the south staircase before study hall.

"Hey," Carter said.

Mattie started to sweat more. "Do you have them?"

"'Course."

Caroline frowned. "Prove it."

Carter opened his backpack. Next to a package of bottle rockets, there were five small boxes. Inside, the crickets chirped away. It sounded like a mini summer swamp.

Carter passed Mattie the first box and Mattie gently shook it. The chorus of chirping grew louder. Mattie had expected his stomach to be knotted and his lungs to be tight and they weren't. In fact, the whole thing felt almost like fun.

Except for the crickets dying in the air vent part. Mattie felt pretty bad about that. "Let's go," he said.

"Eww!" Caroline wrinkled her nose.

"What?"

"You smell like Doyle."

Of course he did. Mattie was wearing Doyle's dirty baseball jersey and hat—both of which had been stolen by Eliot after he lost three rounds of rock, paper, scissors to Mattie.

"I feel bad doing this," Mattie said, tugging at the jersey. "If Eliot doesn't get the cameras turned off and the teachers think Doyle screwed up the air vents, he could get in a lot of trouble."

"Don't feel bad," Carter told him.

Mattie tensed. There was something about the way Carter said *Don't feel bad* that made him suspicious. *"Why?"*

"Focus, Mattie. Not everything is about you." Carter checked his watch. "You really think Eliot can do this?"

"Of course," Mattie said. Mostly, he thought.

"Well, let's get in place, then."

They hovered under the trees, watching the corner security camera. The light would be easier to see in the dark, but if Mattie squinted, he could see the red flash.

Still red . . . still red . . . still— The light vanished and the camera tilted slowly downward as if shutting off.

"He did it!" Mattie breathed. Carter glanced around and then waved for Mattie and Caroline to follow him. Everyone dropped to their hands and knees and scurried into the rosebushes.

"Ow! Ouch! Yow!" everyone cried, *very* quietly, and after a few feet of scrambling, all three popped through to the other side. They crouched in the narrow space between the rosebushes and the gym's outside wall and plucked thorns from their skin. As promised, the air-conditioning unit was right there and Mattie only had to tug a bit to get the top vent hood to loosen. He passed the lid to Caroline.

"Okay," Mattie breathed as he held the first cricket container over the open vent. "Here goes."

"Perfectly good waste of perfectly good crickets," Carter muttered. The crickets chirped and squeaked as Mattie gently shook them into the vent. Their hard, little bodies made tiny tapping noises as they hit the metal frame.

"Sorry, guys." Mattie poured another box of crickets into the vent. "It's for a good cause."

"Oh, yeah," Caroline whispered. "I'm sure that makes all the difference to them." She scooted around to glare at Carter. "Why do all your pranks involve animals anyway?"

"That's not true. When I had Doyle spit in Mattie's soup that didn't involve any animals." Carter paused. "Except for Doyle."

Mattie nearly dropped his cricket box. "You had him spit in my *soup*?"

"Honestly, it didn't take much convincing. He totally hates you." Carter paused, eyes far away as if he were reminiscing. "He really put some effort into it too."

Mattie gagged. "Why does he hate me so much?"

"Who knows? It was something about a sponge." Carter shrugged. "I like to think it's because you bring out the best in people."

Mattie glared. "When did this happen?"

"Don't be so dramatic. It was last term. I haven't done anything to you lately. And"—Carter looked at Caroline, who still looked at Carter as if she would like to set him on fire—"I didn't do anything to that possum. He was dead when I found him."

"And the chickens?"

"They were alive when I dropped them into the cafeteria. What happened after was not my fault."

"What happened after was chicken nuggets," Mattie said

and then wished he hadn't. Caroline's face was already flushed a deep, furious red and Carter grinned like he found the whole thing hilarious.

He probably does, Mattie thought as he picked up another container. "Hey," he whispered.

Carter and Caroline ignored him.

"Hey!"

Carter and Caroline glared at him as Mattie emptied the last box into the vent and replaced the air vent's screen. He waited a moment. "Nothing's happening."

"Of course nothing's happening. Give it a minute." Carter peeked his head out of the rosebush and used some of Mr. Larimore's favorite swear words when the thorns tore at his cheeks. "Okay, it's clear. Let's go—and be cool, you guys. Don't look guilty."

"I know how to pull off a prank," Caroline whispered.

"I wasn't talking to you." Carter jammed his thumb toward Mattie. "I was talking about Captain Do Good back there."

"It's Mattie," Mattie hissed.

"It's Dead Man if this doesn't work."

Mattie scowled. It was annoying when Carter had a good point. He followed his brother and Caroline. They knelt behind the arcade and waited.

And waited.

And waited.

Until . . .

Beep! Beep! Beep! The alarm screeched to life, and two seconds later Lem burst through the gym doors. The scientist tore across the grassy quad as fast as his legs would carry him. "Fire!" he shrieked. "Run for your life!"

The friends leaned forward and watched him go. Carter mumbled under his breath. "No Weather-matic."

The doors flew open again. "Fire!" Two more scientists galloped past, arms waving.

"So dramatic." Carter grinned. "We should have done this weeks ago. I've needed a good laugh."

Mattie really begged to differ. What they *needed* was the Weather-matic. But in their panic, the scientists weren't evacuating the inventions. They were just running away. Mattie chewed the skin next to his thumbnail. What if this didn't work?

"Carter—" Mattie began, but he never got to finish, because as Mattie, Carter, and Caroline watched, the gym exploded.

KNOW WHEN TO GET OUT

MATTIE FELL BACKWARD, LANDING ON HIS BUTT. CAROLINE HIT the dirt and covered her head. And Carter? Well, Carter stared with his mouth open.

"That. Was. Amazing," he finally managed.

Mattie stared up at his brother. Blowing up the school gym was a lot of things, but Mattie didn't think it was amazing. He jumped to his feet and grabbed Carter by the collar. "We were supposed to make everyone think there was a fire, not actually burn down half the school!"

Carter shrugged. "Sometimes my brilliance cannot be contained."

"Did you know that was going to happen?"

"Mattie, I took a calculated risk." Carter paused and

everyone watched as a bucket arced through the hole in the gym roof. It looked like an especially odd rocket. "I'm just really bad at math, so, you know, you get what you get. Anyway, you asked for them to bring you the Weather-matic, and now they are."

Mattie spun around and realized Carter might be right. Dr. Hoo and a few of the other scientists were now dragging inventions onto the lawn. Or, at least, they were dragging things that could be inventions. Mattie had no idea why a shark tank had been in the gym or why four scientists were now hauling that shark tank onto the grass.

Mattie craned his head. "None of these are the Weather-matic."

"So go get it," Caroline said.

"What? How?" And then Mattie saw it. There was a hole in the gym's side now. Not a huge hole, but definitely big enough to crawl through—and see the outlines of machines stored inside.

Mattie pushed to his feet before he lost his nerve. He ran along the wall, keeping inside Munchem's hulking shadow, and then, when he was just across from the hole in the gym's side, he bolted across the smoldering grass.

Inside, the gym was hazy with green smoke. Somewhere to Mattie's left, people were shrieking at each other to move, and somewhere to his right, another alarm was going off. The once-upon-a-time ballroom's gilded walls were now a decidedly smoky brown, and the spidery-armed candelabras were still swinging from the force of the explosion.

Mattie tugged the edge of Doyle's jersey over his nose and mouth—and gagged. *That's worse than the smoke,* he thought, eyes watering as he scrambled over the tubes that lay across the floor. *Where is it? Where is—*

There!

Like a finger jammed toward the sky (which you could now clearly see through the hole in the roof), the Weather-matic's pointed top rose above the smoke. Mattie ran ahead, swatting at his singed pants as he went. He dashed past the giant espresso maker, made a right at a table filled with clown dolls, doubled back at a pot of boiling something, and found it. The Weather-matic was taller than he remembered, and Mattie had to launch himself at it, scrambling up the side.

The Weather-matic wobbled left and then right. Mattie clung to a bright blue power cord and wedged his arm between two electrical panels, fingers straining for the glowing core. He tugged one wire loose and then another. The machine shook so hard Mattie's teeth rattled. It trembled and trembled and then went still.

"Hurry up," Mattie whispered to himself. He pulled off the last connector and yanked the crystal free. It was still warm and fit exactly in the palm of his hand. Mattie shimmied back down and tucked the crystal into his pocket. For something so dangerous, it was awfully light. Mattie could barely feel it thumping against his leg as he ran between inventions.

"You there!" someone yelled.

Someone? It was Dr. Hoo!

"Stop!"

Mattie didn't stop. He went even faster, pumping his knees and elbows as hard as he could.

Almost to the hole. Almost to the hole. Almost— Mattie hurled himself through the gap and hit the singed grass running.

"Stop him!" Dr. Hoo yelled, and if Mattie hadn't been at Munchem, he might very well have been stopped, but because Mattie was at Munchem—a school filled with students who were bad, didn't like to follow rules, and definitely didn't like to follow orders such as being told to stop someone—Mattie escaped. He kept his head down as the students closed in around him, and even though Mattie had to shove to get through them, he made it.

And Dr. Hoo did not.

"Is that Doyle?" someone said as Mattie elbowed past him.

"Too short," someone else said.

"He's getting away!" Dr. Hoo shrieked, still trying to push through the students. The students pushed back. No one was going to help Dr. Hoo catch Doyle. Doyle was like Munchem royalty. "He was inside! Get him!"

Mattie powered across the lawn and spun around the

corner, a pale-faced Caroline falling into stride next to him. She helped Mattie yank off Doyle's jersey and hat, and they tossed them into an empty classroom.

Mattie hustled toward the doors at the end of the hallway, smoothing down his Munchem sweater, and Caroline pulled him to a walk. "Be cool!" she hissed.

"I was nearly set on fire!" Mattie hissed back. He did walk, though, because Caroline was right. They needed to look like they were just two students off to study hall or their dorms or anywhere that wasn't the flaming gym. They passed through the double doors and walked into the sunshine.

"Did you get it?" Caroline ducked her head as two upperclassmen ran past, heading for the fire.

Mattie nodded, still sucking in breaths. Long black snakes of smoke rose above the roofline. "We . . . blew up . . . the gym," Mattie managed.

"Technically, we just blew holes in it."

Caroline was trying to make Mattie feel better. Sadly, she did not. The crystal bumped Mattie's thigh with each step and his lungs were on fire, which, of course, was an extremely unpleasant reminder of what he'd done.

They walked past the school's south entrance, and when they reached one of the courtyards, Mattie flopped down on the closest stone bench, legs shaking. He rubbed his sweaty hands on his knees.

"Here." Caroline pulled off her book bag and tossed

Mattie her American History book. It almost knocked him over. "Look like you're reading until you can get up without passing out."

Part of Mattie wanted to argue, but the rest of him was too busy struggling to breathe. "How did you even run with that in your bag?"

"What do you think? I spent my childhood with Eliot Spencer. I'm very good at running. I had to be to survive."

Beezus squeaked in agreement.

"Where is Eliot anyway?" Mattie looked around. Two more students rushed by, heading for the gym. They were so excited they didn't even look in Mattie and Caroline's direction. "Shouldn't he be here by now?"

Boom!

Mattie and Caroline looked up as something black shot across the tops of Munchem's chimneys.

"What was that?" Mattie asked.

"A chair?"

"Definitely a chair," Eliot announced. Mattie and Caroline turned and spotted him strolling through the courtyard's entrance. Eliot's jacket was straight, his fists were deep in his pockets, and as he made his way toward them, his face was perfectly serene. Eliot didn't look at all like a kid who would use his computer, Marilyn, to help Mattie blow up the gym. In later years, Eliot would call this his Off-to-Sunday-School look.

"That?" Eliot said once he was standing in front of his sister and his best friend. "That was amazing."

Mattie sighed. "Carter thought so too."

"Well, Carter was right."

"Of course I'm right. I'm always right." Carter hopped over the sagging wall and dusted off his hands. Mattie looked from face to face. Just as planned, everyone had met up, and just as planned, Mattie had the crystal.

I really should feel better about this, Mattie thought.

"Okay then." Carter kicked Mattie's sneaker. "Let's see it."

There was no doubt in anyone's mind what *it* was. Mattie spent a moment showing everyone the crystal. He also spent another moment breaking out into a cold sweat because anyone could have walked into that courtyard and Carter didn't care.

"Believe me, Mattie," Carter said, examining the crystal with distinct disappointment. "No one cares about us. They have better stuff going on."

And as if to underscore Carter's point, there was a low boom and another piece of the laboratory wheeled through the air. Everyone paused to stare.

Carter cracked his knuckles. "So what are we going to do with the crystal? Hide it? Sell it?"

Mattie shook his head. There was only one thing they could do with something so powerful. "We have to destroy it."

NEVER GIVE UP

"PLEASE DON'T DO THIS," ELIOT REPEATED AS HE TROTTED ALONG behind Mattie. Smoke still streamed from the gym's rooftop, turning the air gritty. "I'm begging you."

"No way."

"Then destroy it after I get to use it."

"*Definitely* no way."

Above them the loudspeaker screeched to life, and the boys winced. "All students should report to their dorms immediately!" Professor Shelley screamed. "Right now!"

In the distance, sirens whined. Eliot grinned. "This is so cool. They're sending in the fire department."

Mattie groaned. Forget Mr. Larimore's big blue vein—his dad's head was going to explode once he heard about this. "Let's go," Mattie said, dragging Eliot toward their dorm.

They kept close to the school's edge, watching smoke curl upward. "What if you destroy the crystal after I get to study it?" Eliot asked.

"No. Way." Mattie kept going. If he stopped, he might reconsider, and if he reconsidered he might chicken out—or give the crystal to Eliot to experiment with, which was way worse.

Eliot made a gargling noise deep in his throat. "I thought we were friends."

"We *are*."

Eliot muttered something under his breath. Mattie couldn't be sure, but it sounded like "such a downer" and "no one knows how to have a good time around here."

Mattie started to argue but paused as a shadow slipped over them. *What was that?* He slowed, looking up at the second- and third-floor windows, and then the roof above them.

"What is it?" Eliot asked.

"Nothing." *Because I'm seeing things, right? Right,* Mattie decided. "Eliot?" Mattie asked.

"Yeah?"

"This is happening."

Eliot covered his face with both hands and moaned. "Destroy the cloning machine," he whispered as two other students ran past. "Destroy the crystal. Is there *any* scientific advancement you don't feel the need to ruin?"

Mattie thought about it. "The ones that don't hurt people?"

Eliot sighed. "Fine. How should we do it?"

Mattie wasn't sure. If the crystal was powerful enough to run the Weather-matic, what would happen if they broke it? Would it explode like cars in movies? Shatter like glass? Catch fire?

Okay, Mattie knew the last one was a bit of a stretch, but he was jumpy after the gym debacle. Luckily for Mattie, something as small and fragile as the Weather-matic's crystal would be easy to break, right?

Right.

"I think . . ." Mattie began.

"Look out!" Eliot yelled.

Crash! A slate shingle hurtled to the ground, narrowly missing Mattie's head. The boys jumped back, narrowly missing a second shingle flying down to join the first. The boys stared down at the shattered slate. "It's kind of a wonder no one's been killed like this before," Eliot said at last as the sirens climbed and the smoke stung their eyes.

Mattie nodded, toeing the bits of roofing as an idea came to him. "I think I know how we can destroy the crystal."

In the end, Mattie wasn't happy about blowing up the gym, but much like the yellow snow, he was grateful for the chaos. It made for the perfect cover. The professors didn't notice two boys hustling through the meadow below Munchem because they were too busy yelling at one another, and the firefighters didn't notice two boys sneaking past because they were too busy with the smoldering gym. The clones saw them, but that was because they were staring up at the still-smoking school.

"Did you bring me any more of those breakfast sandwiches?" Maxwell asked as soon as Mattie stepped into the cemetery. One eye was brown and the other was red, and Mattie didn't want to know *what* was in his hair.

"Sorry, Maxwell, I had to leave in a hurry. I don't have any food with me."

"Caroline would've remembered," the clone grumbled. Mattie frowned. This was true, but the group had split up after deciding to destroy the crystal. Caroline was probably back in her dorm right now and Carter was, well, wherever Carter felt like going.

Mattie paused, looking around the cemetery for the fattest angel. "That one," he said, pointing to a particularly grouchy girl angel standing on a headstone. Mattie fished the crystal out of his pocket and dropped it on the grass in front of the angel, pushing it back and forth until he was pretty sure he had it in the right spot.

"What's he doing?" Doyle asked Eliot.

"Trying to destroy my hopes and dreams."

Mattie scowled at both of them. "I need to shatter the crystal. Dropping the angel on it should do it," he explained to Eliot.

Or tried to explain. Eliot stood even farther away, arms crossed over his chest. The clones didn't seem impressed with Mattie's plan either, but sometimes that's just the way people respond to genius plans.

Coincidentally, it's also the way they respond to non-genius plans too, but Mattie pushed that thought from his mind.

"I don't know," Eliot said, scratching his head until his pale hair stood up. "Haven't we done enough damage?"

"You want this done, or not?"

Eliot tensed. "Actually—"

"Never mind," Mattie said, checking the angel's alignment with the crystal one last time. "All we have to do is push."

Too bad the angel was heavier than she looked. Mattie pushed. Eliot pushed. Mattie and Eliot pushed together.

"Nothing's happening," Eliot wheezed.

"Try harder!" Mattie managed through clenched teeth. He took a few steps back and then ran forward, ramming his shoulder into the angel's base. "Ow!"

"What did you think would happen?" Eliot asked.

Mattie rubbed his shoulder furiously. "Hey, Doyle? Maxwell? Could you help?"

Doyle and Maxwell sighed, but they did indeed help. The

clones, Eliot, and Mattie backed up several strides and then ran forward with everything they had. They hit the stone base with all their weight and—

Crack! The angel wobbled. The angel tilted.

Whump! The angel went face-first into the grass. Bits of dirt and statue flew up, showering them like confetti.

Mattie grinned as they ran around to pull the broken bits of stone away. The force of the statue's fall had driven the crystal and the angel's face into the ground. Mattie dug around with his fingers.

This is totally going to work, he thought, prying back mud and grass roots. The crystal will be smashed to bits. It'll be . . .

In perfect condition. Mattie stared down at the crystal. Even though it was lying in an angel face–shaped hole, it was still shiny and still smooth. It glimmered at him.

"Huh," Mattie said.

"Yeah," Eliot added, giving the statue a kick. The statue didn't move.

"Mattie?" Doyle asked.

"Yeah?"

"I think you have a problem."

Mattie sat back on his heels, and nodded. He thought so too.

"So, uh, what do we do?" Eliot asked.

Mattie considered the crystal for a long moment. It practically twinkled in his palm, mocking him. How could something so pretty be so deadly? "I don't know," Mattie said at last.

"Well, you better come up with something." Eliot looked at Munchem. The fire trucks' lights backlit the school's three and a half towers in red and white. "We can't hold on to it."

"I could hold on to it," Doyle said.

Mattie shook his head. "No way. I'm not putting you in danger too. Hoo isn't going to stop searching for it. He wants the crystal *and* the clone minions. If he found both of you together, it would be, like, a mad scientist win-win."

"What are minions?" Maxwell asked.

"Nothing," Mattie said quickly. He pocketed the crystal. "There has to be another way."

But even as Mattie said it, he couldn't think of a single one.

A GOOD HIDING PLACE
IS HARD TO FIND

IT'S AMAZING HOW MATTIE'S LIFE JUST KEPT GETTING MORE complicated. Amazing or depressing. Or maybe it's just baffling. How was it possible for *so many things* to go wrong?

I don't know for certain, but I'm pretty sure it's due to gravity, and I'm even more sure it's due to incompetent writers. They ruin everything. Ask me how I know.

In the meantime, however, Mattie and the Spencers needed another plan or maybe a miracle. Probably a miracle. Things were bad.

Mattie rolled the crystal from hand to hand. "How do you think Hoo made this thing? How did he make it work for the Weather-matic? How did he *know* it would work for the Weather-matic? I have questions. Loads."

Eliot frowned. "Yeah, that's usually your problem."

"That and you can't let things go," Caroline added.

"I'm not the only one." Mattie held up the crystal. Roughly the size and shape of a plum, it swallowed all the colors around it, lighting up Mattie's hand with rainbows. "Everyone wants this thing. They're not going to stop."

"Thanks, Captain Obvious."

"I'm thinking out loud."

"If we can't destroy it, we have to hide it, but where? They're searching the whole school."

Caroline petted Beezus. "What about somewhere in the basement?"

"Or the cemetery?" Eliot suggested.

Mattie frowned. "But we've been all over those places. What's to say someone else won't do the same thing? It has to be somewhere no one will find it."

Eliot scratched his neck. "Maybe one of the clones could swallow it."

Caroline gasped. "Eliot, you can't ask them to swallow the crystal!"

"Oh, whatever." Eliot waved his hand at his sister. "You make everything sound horrible when you use that tone of voice." He faced Mattie, and with every word his blue eyes got bigger and rounder. "You should think about it. We don't know how their digestive systems work. This could be a great opportunity to find out—and solve your problem."

"If I wouldn't let them hold on to it, why would I let them swallow it?"

"Then come up with something better."

Mattie wasn't sure he could.

"Face it, Mattie," Caroline said quietly. "There's no good place to hide it. It's Munchem. There are too many people. *Someone* will find it."

"It can't be destroyed and it can't be found," Mattie said slowly. "So that means we need to put it somewhere."

It wasn't the smartest thing Mattie had ever said. He kicked at the ants trying to climb into his sneakers. *I need to hide the crystal where it will never be found, but everyone's looking for it and they won't stop until they find it.* Mattie sat a little straighter. It was that little voice again. The one that had good ideas—and occasionally spectacularly bad ones.

"Guys?" Mattie said.

The Spencers looked at him.

"I'm not going to hide it." Mattie grinned. "I'm going to give it back."

Caroline massaged her forehead. "Not this again!"

"You're going to give it back?" Eliot asked slowly. "I can think of about eleventy billion reasons why that's not a good idea."

Mattie grinned even wider. "It is if they don't have the real crystal."

"Huh?"

"I'm going to clone it."

BUT SOMETIMES THE BEST HIDING PLACES ARE OUT IN THE OPEN

"THINK ABOUT IT," MATTIE CONTINUED. HE LEANED CLOSE TO THE Spencers. Some of this was due to the fact that he didn't want to be heard, but the rest of it was due to the fact that Lem was snoring through study hall and the snores were surprisingly deafening considering Lem was such a slight man. "Let's be totally honest with ourselves," Mattie whispered. "What are Dr. Hoo and General Mills and Miss Maple and Delia going to do? Give up looking for the crystal? Of course not. So we give it back to them—only it won't be the real crystal. It'll be a clone, and when it doesn't work, they'll think the crystal's broken."

Caroline sat up fast enough to startle Beezus. "And they

won't look for the real crystal because they'll think they already have it! That's awesome, Mattie!"

"Or terrible." Eliot frowned and picked at his T-shirt's hem. "How do you know that would even work?"

"I don't," Mattie said. "But the cloning machine creates good kids to replace bad kids, right?"

Eliot shrugged. "Yeah."

"Well, what if it could create a good crystal to replace a bad crystal?"

"That's a stretch."

"Is it?" Mattie asked. "I mean people are made out of carbon and this is made out of carbon. Okay, it's a stretch—but if it works, it'll be brilliant!"

"I think we should try." Caroline tugged Beezus out from under her shirt and scratched his scabby head. Bits of fur drifted through a bright sunbeam and landed on the shiny floor. "It's not like you have any other ideas, Eliot."

Eliot scowled. "Do I get to program the machine?" he asked at last.

"I wouldn't let anyone else," Mattie told him. Although this was mostly because no one else would be able to figure it out.

Eliot's face lit up.

"You'll still need to do something with the original," Caroline reminded Mattie. "If you're not careful, you'll get caught with both crystals."

Mattie nodded. "I know."

"And that would mean twice the trouble."

"I know."

"Like, I don't even know what kind of punishments they'd give you for that, but—"

"Caroline?"

"Yes?"

"I *know*!"

Caroline huffed and spun around in her seat, just in time to see Delia walk into study hall, bringing the stench of sweat and powdered milk with her.

"At least one thing went right," Mattie whispered.

"A little too well," Caroline added. "Sour doesn't even begin to describe how disgusting she smells."

The three friends watched as Delia took a seat at one of the nearby tables. Everyone who was sitting there paused, sniffed, and then scattered. Delia glared at the deserters; then she glared at Mattie and Caroline and Eliot.

Mattie and the Spencers suddenly became very interested in their homework.

Mattie tried to breathe through his mouth, but he could taste Delia's stench too. He tried to breathe through his shirt, but then he smelled wool *and* Delia's stench. His eyes began to water.

"Um . . ." Mattie shoved to his feet. "I forgot something in my dorm."

Eliot also shot up. "Me too. I forgot something too."

"Cowards," Caroline muttered, but the boys were already too far away to hear. They hustled into the hallway, and as Mattie passed a window, a dirt mover started up. The engine rumbled to life and Munchem's walls shook as if the school were giggling. Mattie watched one Larimore Corporation employee point at a big dirt pile while two other Larimore Corporation employees nodded in agreement.

"I wonder how long the new parking lot is going to take, because it seems like all they do is move dirt around and—" Mattie stopped. He stared out the window, thinking hard.

For Mattie, sometimes ideas were like sculpting. He had to work and work at a solution until it finally emerged. But other times, ideas felt like they'd been dropped out of the sky, and as Mattie stared at the bulldozers, an idea dropped into his brain. It was completely formed, like it had just been waiting for him to need it.

"Maybe we don't have to destroy the real crystal," Mattie said. "What if we just buried it?"

Eliot followed his friend's gaze, and when he spotted the giant bulldozer, he wilted a little. "No one would look under the parking lot."

This was a good thing, but Eliot's tone verged ever so slightly on tears. Mattie patted his shoulder as he continued to turn the idea over and over. Below them, the bulldozer ground forward and the other two Larimore Corporation employees started shouting at each other. "Aren't they supposed to start paving tomorrow?"

Eliot's lower lip wobbled. "Yeah."

Mattie grinned. "It's perfect. We just have to get close enough to toss it in."

"You said almost the same thing about blowing up the gym."

"Blowing up the gym wasn't the plan; it was just an unfortunate side effect."

"And also awesome."

Mattie frowned. "We can give the cloned crystal back and the construction crew can pave over the real crystal. It'll be done."

"It'll be gone forever," Eliot said, sounding forlorn.

"Safe," Mattie added. He looked at Eliot. "Tonight?"

Eliot nodded. "Tonight."

For the first time since they had stolen the crystal, Mattie felt his chest loosen. "This is going to be great," he said. "We won't have anything left to worry about."

THERE'S <u>ALWAYS</u> SOMETHING
YOU SHOULD WORRY ABOUT

"WE WON'T HAVE ANYTHING LEFT TO WORRY ABOUT." THIS IS AN example of what people call Famous Last Words. Sometimes, words are Famous Last Words because they really *were* the last words someone said, and those words became famous because they were especially true or especially funny or because that chocolate chip cookie recipe is just too good to take to the grave.

But sometimes, Famous Last Words are called Famous Last Words because they're ironic and the speaker has no idea what he or she just said is spectacularly wrong or delusional or inappropriate or all of the above.

Which is exactly the case here. Mattie figured if he buried the crystal, he'd have nothing left to worry about, and the Spencers agreed because, really, what could go wrong?

Well, a lot apparently. But we will have to pay extra-special attention, because Mattie and the Spencers didn't realize what had gone wrong until it was far too late.

Confused? So were the friends at first. The plan began like so many of Mattie's good ideas: he returned to the basement, which was still dirty, still shadowy, and still a secret. From everyone except us, of course.

Mattie edged the door at the bottom of the stairs open and peered inside. Somewhere, something was dripping, but no one was in sight and the machine was quiet. Mattie waved for the Spencers to follow him and they hurried toward the computer station. Eliot sat down at the spinny chair, hands hovering above the keyboard. For a moment, no one said anything and no one moved.

Eliot should really be moving, Mattie thought. "Um, Eliot? Are you okay?"

"Just give me a minute." Eliot wiped his eyes and sniffled.

Is he crying? Caroline mouthed at Mattie. Mattie nodded. Eliot was indeed crying and Mattie had no idea what to do about that.

"Uh, yeah," Mattie said, trying to sound patient, but unable to keep the squeak from his voice. "We really don't *have* a minute."

Eliot didn't look at them. "You can't rush me. I've waited my whole life to use this thing."

"Oh, please." Caroline took a step forward, looking like she was going to give her brother a thump. "You've only known about it since last term. C'mon, Eliot. Quit with the dramatics."

"*Fine*, I need a minute to figure out how to turn it on again!"

"Oh. Okay, then."

Mattie and Caroline stayed quiet while Eliot tinkered with the computer system. His fingers flew across the keyboard and the computer screen flashed bright blue as it powered up.

Behind them, the smokestacks snorted, the conveyor belt groaned, and . . .

Whoosh!

"Did someone just flush a toilet?" Caroline asked, looking worriedly toward the shadowy ceiling. "I just heard water."

"It's coming through the pipes." Mattie pointed to a stop-sign red tube to their right. It jerked twice as the smokestacks began to pump. "Look!"

Like Caroline could look away—like anyone who might have been standing there could've looked away. There was something about the machine lumbering back to life that was terrifying and exciting . . . and terrifying.

Maaaaah! Maaaaah! The computer powered up. Eliot banged

away on the keyboard as long lines of text scrolled across the screen.

"Okay! I think I've got it!" Eliot jumped up from his chair. "If I remember right, the Rooster pulled this thing and then—"

Eliot tugged on an enormous switch attached to the machine's side. It didn't budge. He tugged again. Still nothing. Mattie and Caroline rushed to help. They pulled. They yanked.

Nothing happened.

"Hey!" Mattie stood back. "All at once, okay?"

They nodded.

"On three," Mattie told them.

They nodded again, and everyone grabbed on. The handle was icy in Mattie's grip. He tightened his fingers. "One-two-three!"

All three of them hauled at the handle. *Pop!* It cranked downward. Everyone landed on their butts as smoke blasted through the stacks and the conveyor belt began to move.

"You ready?" Caroline asked.

Mattie nodded. He shoved to his feet and fumbled for the crystal. His hands were shaky. Now was the moment of truth, the moment they would know if the plan would work.

Mattie placed the crystal on the conveyor belt the same way he'd watched the teachers place Maxwell. Well, not *exactly* the same way the teachers had placed Maxwell. The crystal wasn't tied up and it wasn't whimpering and it definitely didn't take three grown-ups to get it on the conveyor belt, but the sentiment was the same. Mostly the same. Whatever, you get the point.

The conveyor belt chugged forward, hauling the crystal into the cloning machine's wide mouth. Mattie and the Spencers craned their heads, but they lost sight of it after only a moment.

"Is it working?" Caroline asked.

"No idea," Mattie said, sniffing the air. "But I smell burned hair, so that means we just need it to—"

Yowl! The machine screeched and Mattie covered his ears. "That," he yelled. "We needed it to do that!"

Yes indeed, it looked and sounded like everything was working precisely as it should. The smokestacks puffed harder. The computer lights went orange. But when Mattie ran to the other end of the conveyor belt, he couldn't see anything coming toward him. The belt churned and churned and Mattie looked and looked.

"There it is!" Mattie cried. The crystal slowly emerged from the cloning machine. It trundled forward, winking and sparkling like it always did. Just like the original does, Mattie thought, all the breath squeezing right out of him.

If the machine worked the same way it did with students, the clone always came first and the original would come second.

Please let this work, Mattie prayed. *Please let this work*. The conveyor belt kept trundling, and a heartbeat later, the original crystal appeared. Mattie grabbed it. The edges were still warm. He held both crystals up, studying them closely.

"So the original crystal is in your left hand?" Caroline guessed.

"No," Eliot said. "It's in his right."

"No, it's not." Caroline squinted at them and Mattie held his breath. "You know what? I can't tell." She blinked. *"I can't tell!* I can't tell, Mattie! It worked!"

The Spencers jumped up and down and Mattie joined them. "We did it! It worked!"

"Good job," Eliot said, and his smile looked especially shiny under the overhead lights. "This is the easiest thing we've done yet."

Mattie nodded. "Exactly. Like I said, nothing to worry about."

Everyone agreed. Well, everyone except for Delia Dane, who had just crept down the stairs. She looked from Mattie to the Spencers to the machine and smiled.

KNOW WHEN YOU'RE BEATEN

THEY'D DONE IT! THEY'D CLONED THE CRYSTAL! MATTIE KNEW HE was grinning wildly and he couldn't stop. Actually he didn't want to stop grinning. This was amazing. All he had to do now was—

"Give it to me."

Mattie swallowed. It *couldn't* be. Ever so slowly, he began to turn. *Please, please, please don't let it be . . .*

Delia.

Delia stood next to the conveyor belt. Her hair was shiny, her smile was wide, and her jacket was dirt-smeared. "Miss me?"

"Not really," Mattie said, pocketing the crystals. "Want to go away so we can see if I do?"

"Funny." Delia strode toward him, hand outstretched. "Give me the crystal."

"No."

"Yes!"

"No!" Mattie drew himself up and squared his shoulders. It didn't really help. Delia was still two inches taller, but he felt better. "We know about General Mills *and* Miss Maple *and* the lightning setting *and* what you're going to do with the Weather-matic!"

"We do?" Eliot whispered to his sister.

"Shut up!" Caroline whispered back.

Okay, so they didn't know exactly what Delia had planned for the Weather-matic and the crystal, but Mattie was pretty sure whatever Delia had in mind would be bad. Actually, he was positive it would be bad.

He was also positive something had just moved in the shadows behind Delia. Mattie tried not to look. Maybe it was a teacher!

Or maybe it's Dr. Hoo, the little voice inside his head said.

Mattie took a shaky breath. "There is *zero* chance I'm giving you the crystal," he told Delia.

"Oh," she said airily, "I think there's a very good chance you're going to give it to me. In fact, there are two very *big* reasons you're going to do it too."

"Oh, yeah?" Mattie asked.

Delia smirked. "Yeah." She snapped her fingers and Doyle

and Maxwell emerged from the shadows. Doyle pounded one fist into his hand and Maxwell cracked his knuckles.

Mattie felt all the blood drain from his face. Delia was quite right. Doyle and Maxwell *were* indeed very big reasons to give her the crystal.

Caroline brushed past Mattie. She stood in front of him, hands on hips and hair twice the size of her head. "We can take them. There are four of us."

"Beezus doesn't count," her brother whispered furiously. "Stop acting like he does!"

Delia's eyes narrowed. "Get them!"

Maxwell and Doyle jumped forward with a roar. Eliot squeaked, Caroline charged, and Mattie grabbed the back of her shirt. "Stop!" he yelled.

To Mattie's shock, everyone did.

Mattie took a deep breath. "You have to tell me why, Delia!"

She stared at him. "What?"

Mattie tightened his grip on Caroline's shirt as the shadows behind Delia rolled. "Tell me why you want the crystal."

A slow smile crossed Delia's face. She stepped closer to the cloning machine and orange lights from the electrical board rippled across her shiny hair. "Why, Mattie, I'm so glad you asked."

"I'm not! Now she'll never shut up!" Caroline lunged forward again and Mattie hauled her back. The shadows behind

Delia moved once more and Mattie's heart leaped. He *knew* someone was there.

Someone who would help them?

Or someone who would help Delia?

Maxwell growled and started toward them. Delia put a hand on his sleeve. "I'll let you pummel her later," Delia told him. She turned back to Mattie. "You see, I was sent here to fulfill my aunt's latest master plan—you ruined the last one, Mattie—and, frankly I was angry. Gathering up clones for Dr. Hoo? Being stuck here until the Weather-matic was ready? I had way better things to do than watch him accidentally set off thunderstorms in class. In fact, I had so many way better things, it got me thinking about clones. If I had one, I could make it do my homework, my chores. I mean, who *wouldn't* want a minion?"

Eliot sighed, nodding. "Exactly."

"I'm going to thump him," Caroline muttered. Mattie held on to her and watched the shadows. Nothing happened. Was that a good sign? A bad sign? Mattie didn't know, but he did know the longer Delia talked, the better Mattie's chances were of thinking of something—anything—to get them out of this.

"A Delia clone would make me look like the perfect niece," Delia continued, smiling to herself and staring at the machine. "And *that* got me thinking about perfect aunts. You see, my auntie has missed every ballet recital, every school play, every award ceremony I've ever had, and I'm tired of it. Was tired of it. I've moved on. I've *evolved*. I'm not interested in making my aunt love me."

Mattie hesitated. "Well, that's very mature of you."

"Isn't it?" Delia studied the cloning machine's pipes and wires and smokestacks. "Now, I'm interested in making the whole *world* love me—or fear me. I'm happy with either."

Mattie's stomach lowered an inch and then one more. This was even worse than they thought. "That's why you want the Weather-matic? To threaten people into doing what you want?"

"Not just people. Governments. Countries. Entire continents!" Delia turned back to Mattie, looking at him expectantly. "What do you think of that?"

I think I see a very bald head poking around the smokestack! Mattie blinked, sure he was hallucinating, but he wasn't. It was Doyle—the clone that is—creeping along the top of the machine.

What's he doing?

Clone Doyle crept from pipe to pipe, frame to frame, without a single sound, and when the Spencers inhaled hard, Mattie knew they'd seen the clone too.

"Well?" Delia demanded. "What do you think?"

"I think you sure do like to talk about yourself," Mattie said.

Delia scowled like he had let her down.

It was sort of true. You see, at this point in his life, Mattie didn't know the rules of villains and heroes and heroes who were also thieves. He had no idea that when Delia the Terrible was talking, he was supposed to listen—and be suitably scared. This is part of Hero-Villain Statute 747B: Villain Monologues.

"Of course I like to talk about myself," Delia managed through clenched teeth. Eyes bulging, Real Doyle and Real Maxwell looked at each other. Mattie and the Spencers weren't the only kids scared of Delia. "I'm *fascinating*."

Clone Doyle dangled twenty feet above her head, and when Mattie's eyes widened, she grinned. "I know. I'm terrifying too. It's a gift."

"Well, I still don't get it," Mattie said.

"What?" Delia frowned as Clone Doyle swung on an antenna, his mud-caked shoes dancing. "*Why?* I explained everything perfectly."

"Well, *yeah*. You explained that part, but not the rest." Mattie tried very hard not to look at Clone Doyle, who was still dangling from the antenna. "How did Miss Maple even know about the Weather-matic? And how did she meet Dr. Hoo?"

Delia slumped. Clearly, her big moment wasn't nearly as satisfying when Mattie played dumb. "They met online," she said finally. "There are websites for everything—including world domination. Hoo told her all about the Weather-matic. They were supposed to be partners, but then he double-crossed her."

Mattie thought for a moment. "Did you know about that when you caught me in the headmaster's office?"

Delia's expression darkened. "I didn't then, but I do now, and *now* I'm taking over." She smiled her nastiest smile, and even though Mattie was trying to be tougher, he couldn't stop shivering at the sight. "I want that crystal, Mattie. Both of them."

"Too bad." Mattie thought he sounded awfully determined for someone whose insides had gone liquid. "You can't have them."

Delia paused. "If you don't give it to me, I really will destroy you. Purple glitter and shredded Dream Bears were just playing around."

"I can take it." Again, Mattie sounded brave.

Delia's eyes narrowed. "Fine. If you don't give it to me, I'll destroy *them*." Delia didn't point or even look at Caroline and Eliot. She didn't have to. Mattie knew exactly whom she meant. "Maxwell and Doyle will turn them into pulp and it will be *your* fault."

Everyone fell silent. There was only the hum of generators and the drip of pipes. If anyone could make good on that promise, it was Delia Dane. Mattie knew it, the Spencers knew it, and Delia especially knew it.

"Face it," she said. "You're done. I beat you."

Mattie looked at Delia. He looked at Caroline and Eliot. Then he looked at Real Maxwell and Real Doyle and tried *not* to look at the clone dangling above their heads. Mattie had to admit Delia was right. They were caught. It was a depressing realization.

It also gave him an idea.

"You're right," Mattie said, sliding his hand into his pocket. He pulled out the crystals and rolled them around in his palm.

Caroline gasped. "Mattie! Don't!"

"You can't!" Eliot yelled.

"I have to! Delia's right. She won." Mattie tossed the crystals at Delia. "Here. Take them."

Delia snatched the crystals from the air. "This is why you shouldn't have friends, Mattie. They make you weak." She paused, peering down at her hand. "Wait. Which one's the real crystal?"

"Guess you'll find out," Mattie replied.

"Bu-but if I pick wrong, the machine could be ruined!"

"Oh darn, that's right," Mattie said.

Delia glared at him before spinning around. "Have fun," she said to Real Maxwell and Real Doyle. The Reals—as Mattie was beginning to think of them—rubbed their hands together.

"Hey!" Mattie yelled. "A deal's a deal! I gave you the crystals!"

But Delia was already gone.

IF YOU CAN'T DAZZLE THEM
WITH BRILLIANCE THEN CON THEM
WITH CLONES

WELL, SHE WASN'T *EXACTLY* ALREADY GONE. MATTIE AND THE
Spencers listened to Delia's footsteps as she ran across the concrete floor and up the concrete steps. They were light and fast
footsteps and they disappeared somewhere around the ladder,
growing softer and softer until they were nothing at all.

"Which one do you want to punch first?" Real Doyle asked
Real Maxwell, stepping forward. His feet scraped against the
cold concrete floor.

"The girl one," Real Maxwell said.

Caroline sighed. "Well, you can *try*," she said. As far as
heroic responses to being punched go, it was a pretty good
quip. But, honestly? There wasn't much heart in it.

Mattie understood. This wasn't their best moment. He

needed another idea—a really good one too, because Real
Maxwell and Real Doyle had started toward them. Mattie and
the Spencers backed up.

"Get them!" Real Doyle shouted.

"Run!" Mattie yelled. Eliot scrambled across the conveyor belt. Mattie and Caroline dove under the fat red pipes.
Maxwell went after Eliot. Doyle chased Mattie and Caroline.

"How could you give Delia the crystal?" Caroline scurried
along on her hands and knees. "She's going to hurt people!"

"No, she's not," Mattie said, crawling along after her. They
wedged themselves between two support columns as Doyle
puffed behind them.

"Come here!" he shouted.

"Highly unlikely!" Caroline shouted back.

"This way!" Mattie yanked her toward a set of metal stairs.
They led up to another platform and the platform led . . . actually Mattie had no idea. He'd deal with it in a minute.

Caroline and Mattie reached the top step and spun right.
They hit a wall. They spun back around, and galloped across
the platform and around a corner and—

"We are so screwed," Caroline said, panting.

She was right. The platform dead-ended into a massive
electrical cabinet. There was no going over. There was no
going under. They were caught.

"Ow!" Eliot shrieked. Mattie cringed. It sounded like Eliot
was caught too.

"Gotcha," Doyle said. Mattie and Caroline swung around. Doyle flexed his meaty hands. "Now, who wants to go first?"

Whap!

Clone Doyle dropped in front of Real Doyle. "I do!" he announced.

Real Doyle's mouth fell open. His eyes went huge. "I—I—I—"

"Am a horrible human being," Caroline muttered.

Mattie elbowed her.

"What is this?" Real Doyle squealed. Mattie nearly laughed. Relief and panic were warring inside him, and it made Real Doyle's high-pitched squeak way funnier than it should've been.

"It's a long story," Mattie told Real Doyle. "Hey, Doyle?"

Both Doyles turned.

"Uh." Mattie glanced at Caroline and she shrugged. "Doyle the clone?"

"What?" Real Doyle asked. His voice was even squeakier.

"Yes?" Clone Doyle asked Mattie.

"Could you keep him here for us? We have to save El—"

Bam!

Eliot hurtled around the corner. "Guys! Maxwell saved me from himself!"

But apparently not before Real Maxwell had punched Eliot in the face. His cheek was purpling. "This is even better than the gym blowing up! I have a bodyguard!"

"You're going to need one if Delia gets ahold of the Weather-matic," Caroline said, bending in half as she caught her breath.

"Maybe not," Mattie managed. He needed to explain and he didn't have the breath. Nearly dying always did that to him. "Fifty-fifty chance Delia picks the wrong crystal."

Caroline thumped him. "Fifty-fifty chance she picks the right one!"

"What's going on?" Real Doyle's face was shiny with sweat. He couldn't drag his eyes from Clone Doyle. "Why does he look like me?"

Mattie ignored him. "What does 'destroy the machine' mean anyway? If Delia *does* use the wrong crystal, what happens?"

"Don't know," Caroline said.

Eliot clapped his hands together. "So let's go find out!"

"Clone Doyle?" Mattie looked at the clone. "Can you keep them here?"

"Sure! And take some muffins to go!"

Mattie frowned. "But there aren't any—"

Caroline held up her empty hand. "Yum! Yum!" she said, pretending to eat.

Clone Doyle's nose wrinkled. "Is she okay?" he asked Mattie. "Because there's nothing in her hand."

"I'll get her checked out," Mattie said, dragging the Spencers with him. "We'll be right back!"

Mattie didn't think he'd ever run so fast in his life. He took the stairs two at a time. He scrambled up the ladder. He ran flat-out across the overgrown meadow and didn't trip once, which was quite the feat considering how the moon had ducked behind the clouds and shadows pooled everywhere.

But even all of this wasn't enough for Mattie to catch up to Delia.

"She'll head for the gym!" Caroline shouted, ponytail whipping behind her.

"Wait!" Eliot cried, running behind them. "What are you going to do, Mattie?"

Mattie had no idea. Like running from Maxwell and Doyle, some things had to be figured out as they happened. Or at least Mattie hoped he would figure it out as it happened. Honestly, all this was far too much to explain while running across the Munchem campus.

Mattie and the Spencers dashed across the still-crispy lawn, dodging half-burned inventions, a very un-burned shark tank, and . . . Dr. Hoo and Professor Shelley?

Mattie and the Spencers skidded to a stop as the two scientists wrestled across the grass in front of the gym. "I won't let you do this!" Professor Shelley cried. "It's over!"

"Aargh!" Dr. Hoo bellowed, not because he agreed, but because Professor Shelley had him by the hair and was yanking as hard as she could.

"Lem!" Professor Shelley yelled. "Lem, c'mon!"

Lem was indeed coming. The tall, thin scientist barreled out of the dark toward Hoo and Shelley. "Students!" Lem cried, noticing Mattie, Caroline, and Eliot looking on. "Don't! Move! He isn't who you think!"

"Who?" Caroline asked.

"Hoo!" Lem flung himself on top of Professor Shelley and Dr. Hoo. They wrestled right. They wrestled left. They didn't notice the ballroom-turned-gym's windows brightening up, or the hole from the explosion beginning to illuminate with pink.

Mattie gasped. He looked from the wrestling teachers to the hole in the wall, and back to the teachers. There was no time to wait. Mattie hurled himself forward. The Spencers charged after him. And Professor Shelley, under a pile of arms and legs, threatened to give everyone detention.

Inside, all the lights were blazing. Mattie couldn't see a thing—and then he could. Specifically, he could see Delia climbing up the side of the Weather-matic.

"Delia! Stop!" Mattie cried. "Please!"

Delia didn't stop. If anything, she climbed faster. Hand over hand, foot over foot, Delia grabbed the Weather-matic's wire antenna and swung a few feet higher. Mattie groaned and pumped his legs harder. The Spencers were close behind him.

Just a little farther, Mattie thought, his lungs on fire. *Keep going!*

Mattie, Caroline, and Eliot did keep going—until bright orange light shot up toward the ceiling. Mattie slid to a stop. Caroline, then Eliot, crashed into him. The orange light widened and then narrowed, focusing.

Mattie gasped. "She found the right one! She's going to use it!"

Eliot grabbed his arm. "Then we need to go!"

"WHAT?"

Caroline grabbed Mattie's other arm. "He's right! We have to get out of here!"

The Weather-matic began to shake. Its belly turned red.

"You know how this ends, Mattie!" Caroline yelled, pulling Mattie with all her strength.

He yanked his arm from her grip. "Of course I do! That's why we have to stop her!"

Boom!

The orange beam shot a fresh hole in the gym roof. Mattie and the Spencers hit the floor, covering their heads with their arms.

"Delia?" Mattie yelled. There was no answer. Mattie peeked up at the Weather-matic. The top of Delia's shiny blond head poked out of the machine.

The sound of buttons being tapped rippled down toward them. Mattie shuddered. *She's going to fire the Weather-matic again!*

"Delia!" Mattie shouted again. The tarnished candelabras trembled. Bits of glass and plaster started to fall. "You don't want to do this!"

"Oh, yes she does," Caroline said.

Eliot leaned closer to Mattie. "You still haven't told us what you're going to do." Mattie frowned. The color drained from Eliot's face. "I thought you knew what you were doing!"

Mattie stood up. Plaster crunched beneath his sneakers. "I have an idea. It just might not be a good one." He faced the Weather-matic and cleared his throat. "*Delia*," Mattie said in his deepest voice, the one he thought made him sound a little like Mr. Larimore right before he made an employee cry. "That's enough. Come down here right now."

Delia peered at Mattie from over the Weather-matic's top. For a second, she seemed to consider coming down. For a second, she seemed to agree it had been enough.

But it was only for a second.

Delia aimed the Weather-matic straight at Mattie and fired.

GO OUT WITH A BANG

THE GYM WENT BRIGHT, BRIGHT, *BRIGHT.* THE FLOOR SHOOK. MATTIE squeezed his eyes shut and waited to be blown into a bazillion pieces.

Mattie waited . . . and waited.

Nothing's happening.

He opened his eyes and looked around. The gym was still standing, the Weather-matic was still running, and Delia was . . . standing under a rain cloud?

She glared up at it. "Get them!" Delia pointed in Mattie's direction. "Zap him!"

The pony-size cloud rumbled.

"Uh-oh," Mattie breathed.

The cloud crackled. Tiny forks of lightning shot up as

rain dripped down. Delia shielded her hair. "Not *me*! *Them!*"

BOOM! Thunder rolled across the gym and—*WHOOSH!*—more rain coursed down, soaking Delia.

"Stop yelling at it!" Mattie cried. "You're only making it worse!"

Behind him, Caroline made a disgusted noise. "Like she'll be able to stop. Shutting up is Delia's kryptonite. She'll keep going until it drowns her."

"That's not how kryptonite works."

"Look at that and tell me it's not working." Caroline pointed to the cloud and Mattie had to admit: yes, indeed, it was working. Delia was yelling. The cloud was raining. Things were not working out the way Mattie's archnemesis had planned.

"I don't get it," Eliot said. "Is the Weather-matic broken?"

Mattie shook his head. "If the original crystal made the weather go *away* from the Weather-matic's user, the cloned crystal must make it *return* to the user!" Mattie sagged with relief. He almost laughed. Almost. "She's using the wrong crystal!"

"Delia is doomed." Eliot was pretty much entirely correct. The cloud billowed around Delia's head, going pink and orange with lightning. Delia ducked. The cloud followed.

Caroline laughed. "Sorry," she said to Mattie. Caroline wasn't really sorry. She was cracking up, and in her defense, it was rather funny. Or really funny. Take your pick.

In my personal, highly educated opinion, though, it will always be amusing to watch angry purple clouds follow someone around. Especially when that person is Delia Dane. And *especially* when Delia Dane has told your publishers that you might not know as much as you think you do.

I'm petty like that. Plus, Delia's *wrong*. I know loads—like, for instance, I know at this moment, she's never been so wet.

Delia whapped the machine with her hand, shivering. "Stupid! Stupid! Stupid!"

Mattie straightened. "Someone better go get a teacher."

BOOM!

Delia's thundercloud rippled with lightning.

Mattie paled. "Like *now*!"

Caroline jumped to her feet, ready to dash for the hole. But because this is Munchem, things always get worse. Delia's cloud rained harder and swirled faster and grew longer and—

"It's forming a funnel," Mattie breathed, barely able to force out the words.

The cloud reached toward the once-gilded ceiling and pushed down toward the floor. It snaked left and then right and then left again, spiraling around and around Delia so she couldn't escape.

"Tornado!" Mattie yelled, wind buffeting him from all sides.

Eliot ducked as a tarnished candelabra plunged from the ceiling. "What do we do?"

"*Nothing!* You stay right there, Eliot Spencer!"

Professor Shelley scaled the rubble, her black cardigan

flapping like a cape. Her eyes were pinned on Delia. Mattie couldn't believe what he was seeing. Professor Shelley was going to save Delia. Even after Delia blackmailed her. Even after Delia was . . . well, *Delia.*

Personally, I would've left her, but Professor Shelley didn't. She charged past the wreckage, leaned into the wind, and grabbed for Delia's legs as the tornado sucked her into the air.

Taking Professor Shelley with it.

"Aiiieee!"

Delia and Professor Shelley screamed as the tornado sucked them higher.

"Stop the Weather-matic!" Mattie yelled, running toward the machine. The Spencers were right behind him. Eliot grabbed the keyboard and tentatively pressed a few buttons. Delia and Professor Shelley went higher.

"Whoops," Eliot muttered, pressing a few more. "Tell me what's happening. I can't watch!"

Mattie and Caroline couldn't look away. Delia and Professor Shelley swirled higher and higher. *It isn't working.* Mattie panicked. *We have to do something!*

But what? Mattie looked from the Weather-matic to Eliot to the floor to the soggy diaper lying *on* the floor.

Soggy diaper?! It was the Aluminum Falcon! Mattie leaped for it, grabbing its coffee can–size engines with both hands.

"Is that the Falcon?" Caroline cried, shielding Beezus from the flying bits of ballroom. "What are you doing?"

Mattie wasn't sure. The Aluminum Falcon hadn't worked that great even before it was sodden from the sprinkler system, but after stabbing a few buttons (okay, fine, he stabbed all the buttons), it sputtered to life, hovering over Mattie's lap.

He tugged at the concrete gray fabric. If Delia and Professor Shelley grabbed the Falcon, would it hold? What if he—

"Aiiieee!" Professor Shelley and Delia screamed. They were almost at the ceiling. They were almost *through* the ceiling!

"The crystal!" Eliot yelled, clinging to the Weather-matic's side as the wind buffeted him. "If we break the machine's connection with the crystal, it will lose power!"

And *that* was when Mattie got a better idea. Eliot was right: the Weather-matic channeled its power through the crystal. If Mattie could interrupt that with something—something like an Aluminum Falcon—maybe they could stop the funnel.

"I really hope this works," Mattie muttered, programming in the coordinates just like he'd watched Lem do all those months before. The Falcon sputtered. The Falcon sparked. The Falcon took off!

The wind spun it in circles, and dipped it up and down, but the Falcon chugged on. It flew alongside the Weather-matic's cherry red potbelly, it putt-putted past the brackets holding the crystal, and then—

PLOP!

The Falcon smothered the crystal in its wet, diapery folds.

The Weather-matic chugged twice. Its potbelly began to dim. The wind swirled harder, and then slowed.

And stopped.

And Professor Shelley and Delia plummeted.

"Aaaaaaaahhhhh!"

They're going to splatter! Mattie thought. *They're going to—*

ZING!

Professor Shelley caught the Weather-matic's crooked antenna with one hand and grabbed Delia with the other. They twisted slowly back and forth as the wind died. Professor Shelley looked furious. Delia also looked furious.

They also looked like they'd fallen out of an airplane. Professor Shelley's hair stuck straight up and Delia's Power Hair was no more.

Delia glared down at Mattie and shook her fist. "I'll get you for this, Mattie Larimore! It isn't over!"

"Delia?" Mattie said. "I think you need to know when you're beaten."

YOUR BIOGRAPHER
KNOWS BEST

AND *THAT* IS HOW MATHIAS LITTLETON LARIMORE SAVED THE world from Delia Dane and a dangerous Weather-matic and helped re-tank a genetically modified shark—okay, technically that came later, but at the moment, victory was sweet.

And also a bit smoky, Mattie thought, coughing. He waved one hand in front of his face as a piece of once-gilded ballroom ceiling crashed to the floor. "I can't believe the Falcon was finally useful."

"No kidding," someone said. Everyone turned to see Lem shuffling toward them. "I'm so glad you three are okay. I'm not happy you ran in here, but I *am* happy it worked out." Lem looked down at Mattie like he was seeing him for the first time. "I had no idea you had it in you, Mattie."

"No one ever does," Caroline said, wiping ash from Beezus's coat.

Maybe she's right? Mattie thought. This whole semester everyone had been trying to make Mattie into something else. His dad wanted a good kid, Carter wanted a bad brother, and Mattie wanted . . . well, he wasn't sure. He wanted to do the right thing, but sometimes that broke some rules.

Sometimes it broke a lot of rules. Another piece of ceiling whumped to the ground and Mattie toed it. Maybe he was going to have to figure out what was right for him. Maybe that was the real trick to everything.

"Glad I could help," Mattie said finally. Lem nodded, staring from the Weather-matic (smoking) to the Aluminum Falcon (also smoking) to Mattie and the Spencers.

"Your father's going to fire both of us for this," he said at last, his attention straying to Professor Shelley, who was currently telling the police all about why she'd tied up Delia and Dr. Hoo. "This is a disaster, an utter failure—"

"A great opportunity," Mattie said.

Lem's face scrunched up. "Did you hit your head again?"

Mattie looked around. Parts of the gym floor were smoldering, several inventions had melted, and bits of slimy somethings were hanging from the ceiling. The Munchem-ballroom-turned-Munchem-gym had turned to a Munchem disaster area.

"You haven't failed," Mattie said at last. "You found a way to make personal weather machines."

Lem went still.

"Think about it," Mattie continued, lowering his voice to sound like a television announcer. "Do you get hot? Cold? Do you enjoy your showers au naturel? Then you need the Weather-matic!"

Lem backed up a step and took a deep breath. "Finally," Lem boomed, turning his own voice into something suitably announcer-like. "You can have weather that reflects *your* mood, not the world's!"

"Exactly!" Mattie agreed. "But Lem? You probably want to do something about those crystals. The real one, and the, uh, cloned one."

"Cloned one?"

"It's a long story," Mattie said.

"Huh. Well, don't worry. Professor Shelley and I are going to take special care of any and all crystals. In the meantime"—Lem's eyes went bright—"who cares if it rains on your vacation? Who cares if it's cloudy? Because for *you*, it will always be sunny!"

Mattie laughed. "Tell my dad exactly *that*."

Which, of course, was precisely what Lem did. The Larimore Corporation made millions, Lem got a promotion, Dr. Hoo got fired, and Professor Shelley *still* got to keep her job because she had an idea for an even bigger and better computer.

It was almost as good as when Mattie realized the Clones were shadowing the Reals. "I've always wanted my own person," Clone Doyle told Mattie as he hugged Real Doyle. Real Doyle's eyes were huge.

"You'll get used to it," Mattie assured him.

"And just think! You can be good from now on!" Clone Doyle continued, hugging Real Doyle harder. "We can be good together!"

"Yippee?" Real Doyle ventured.

"Who would've thought everything would turn out this well?" Mattie asked the Spencers as they walked to study hall weeks later. The sun was shining, the stone angel was upright and lipstick-free, and Delia Dane was far, far away.

"Maybe things *can* get better at Munchem," Mattie said. Caroline and Eliot nodded. It seemed like Mattie was right.

Personally though I knew he was wrong—because Miss Maple was still out there, and Delia Dane still wanted revenge, and there was *still* a tiny carload of clowns in Mattie's future. Honestly, the burden of always being this knowledgeable weighs on me sometimes.

"Yep," Mattie said, opening one of Munchem's heavy oak doors. "We have nothing left to worry about."

Which of course *everyone* knows isn't remotely true, but that's another story.

ACKNOWLEDGMENTS

Although it will shock his fans around the world, the Commander knows he wouldn't be the Commander without his team at Disney • Hyperion, and he *especially* wouldn't be the Commander without his long-suffering editor, Tracey Keevan, and his equally long-suffering Wonder Agent, Sarah Davies. The Commander salutes you, ladies. Thank you for everything.

For technical research, support, and saucy running commentary, the Commander owes his sidekick, Boy Genius, many medals of service.

And, finally, innumerable thanks go to the Commander's parents; he wouldn't have pulled this off without you.